WRITERS REPUBLIC

TERROR OF
KRONOS

WYATT WELKER

WRITERS REPUBLIC L.L.C.
515 Summit Ave. Unit R1
Union City, NJ 07087, USA

Website: *www.writersrepublic.com*
Hotline: *1-877-656-6838*
Email: *info@writersrepublic.com*

Ordering Information:
Quantity sales. Special discounts are available on quantity purchases by corporations, associations, and others. For details, contact the publisher at the address above.

Library of Congress Control Number: 2022910796
ISBN-13:   979-8-88536-600-7   [Paperback Edition]
                    979-8-88536-659-5   [Hardback Edition]
                    979-8-88536-601-4   [Digital Edition]

Rev. date: 06/13/2022

CONTENTS

CHAPTER

1

LIFE AND DEATH

A boy stands in a large white room, void of everything. He looks down seeing the floor flooded with blood. "How did this happen? What caused so much pain and anger?" He looks around the room seeing two statues, one on both sides. The statue to his right was a cloaked figure with a sword. The other statue is another cloaked figure with a shield instead. "Have I been doing right by the people, my friends, those who died for me?" The statues move closer to him. "Where will this all end? When will peace come....I must think... so hard to think." He sits down in a chair that appears right behind him. "Must think, must remember." A woman's voice is heard. "Let me help you. Just wake up."

The boy wakes in a classroom. Wearing a leather jacket and a blue hat with bull horns on it. He sits up taking his hat off and slicking back his brown hair. Putting his hat back on, two arms wrap around him and he hears the same voice. "Sleep well Markus?" He smiles and sees the girl behind him giggling. "Why didn't you wake me?" She moves over to sit by him and lays her head on his shoulder. "You look so adorable sleeping. You even mumbled something." He rubs her head, smiling until he hears another guy yell "Markus Mars and Sasha Edwards!" Markus sees a black man with a beanie and short beard walking over. "Well I'll be, is that you DJ?" Markus stands up and hugs his friend. "How long has it been?" He asks DJ. "Since middle school dude, ha we got in so much trouble." They laugh as Sasha gets up and hugs DJ "Dany, so good to see you. What brings you to Griffin High? Are you completing your senior year here?" DJ laughs "how did you know?" They laughed and enjoyed seeing each other once again. Their teacher walks in and has everyone settle down. The school day was over before anyone knew it. Markus was sitting in front of the school with DJ. "So Markus, you and Sasha getting it on?" Markus laughs and shakes his head. "No, we want to take it slow, besides she wants to go into art school. Maybe she'll be the next great artist." "Alright, are you still planning on taking over your dad's company? Mars International." Markus looks at the towers in the nearby city. "It's Mars Tech Corporated, or MTC as my mom calls it. And yes. I believe this company can be a good start to helping the world, maybe we will cure cancer, or maybe solve world hunger." He laughs jokingly. "Though it can help bring happiness." A limo pulls up to the school and a young man gets out. "Little Mark, your father wants you to visit him. Come on." Markus rolls his eyes and fist bumps DJ waving bye as he gets into the limo. They drove towards a towering building with the sign labeled 'MTC: providing the future of Mankind.' The drive was silent, they said nothing to one another. Markus looks out the window with a bored look in his eyes. After arriving, Markus walks into the building taking an elevator to the top floor. Upon the door opening a few men in business attire looked at Markus and entered the elevator. As Markus walks out one of the men scoffs at him, yet before the doors shut, Markus sees his face. The man had a scar on his cheek, slicked back blond hair, and a strange look in his eyes. "Killers". Markus heard a creepy raspy voice, with a hint of something in its throat. Markus swings around with a concerned and scared look, breathing heavily. "Is...is anyone there?" A woman walks over. "Young Markus, are you ok? You look like you saw a ghost." Markus returns to a bored look and wipes his face. "No I'm fine, just strange that my father would let such men in." The woman sighs and goes back to her desk with Markus following. "Yes, your father has been inviting some odd company within the last few months... though I'm used to it now." Markus gives a concerned look about what he heard. The secretary remembers "Oh right your father is waiting for you." Markus nods and thanks her before entering the room. The shades were drawn and the room was dark as his father looked out through the blinds. Markus sees his father, how he stood at the window in an authoritative manner. "Markus, how are you, my boy." He says, still staring out the window. "I'm fine dad, just curious about those guys who just left." With a quick reaction his father dismisses the men. "They are nothing special. Ahem. So how is school?" Markus walks towards a chair pulling it out and sitting down. "Well I am doing good in class. Oh my old friend Dany is back." Markus' father walks towards his desk, still not facing his son. He then sits and turns to his computer. "Perhaps you should leave school, become a member of my staff and learn how to lead this company." Markus looks at his father surprised, yet he feels something strange. He notices the room getting a bit chilly. Markus, looking down, upset at the idea says "I think I'm fine in school. Plus there is college too." Markus looks to his father only to see an angered look in his eyes. A look Markus had never seen before. The look in his father's eyes, normally so calm and centered, sends a cold chill down his spine. His father stands up and says, in a commanding voice. "You will not be attending school further. Starting today." Markus was confused. Why would his father forbid him from going to school, why force him out of school? So many questions entered his mind as he left his father's office in a shakened manner. On his way home he thought of how to tell his friends. His house was a story building and looked a lot like a manor, with a goldish colored paint on the interior. Throughout the day he sat around thinking of his girlfriend and his friends. "Sasha..." he whispered her name. Markus felt ill having to leave her. And before the night was through he decided to go to school, no matter his father's wishes. "Screw it, I'm going to school, only to say goodbye. Maybe I'll find a way to stay in school." He says firmly and lays in bed, over the covers looking at a picture on his phone of Sasha, Dany, and himself.

Suddenly a low raspy voice echoes in his mind. "Master... betrayal... pain..." Markus wakes after hearing the voice, just before the alarm for five o'clock rings out. He rubs his head as he goes down stairs. He turns the TV on and the morning news is talking about the weather. Working away in the kitchen Markus cooks up some pancakes. While cooking he gets a call from Dany. "Hey DJ, what's up?" Markus says. happy to hear from him. DJ responded with joy. "Haha. Hey Markus, can't wait for school, it has been so long since we got together." As they joke about their past the news broadcasts an important update. "Earlier today, a bank was robbed, the police are searching for the unknown robbers. Police have not released any information on the bank workers..." As the news continues its report Markus walks out chatting with DJ.

An hour later Markus, DJ, and Sasha are hanging out in the hallway, overjoyed and having so much fun. Markus could only think of how much trouble they would get in when they were younger. "Remember when we barricaded the science room so we could complete our epic science project?" Sasha slaps Markus in the back of his head. "Oh I remember that too, you two got in so much trouble. I'm always gonna be upset about that." Markus feels the back of his head "ouch" but he smiles and DJ sits there laughing. The bells rang and the three felt a wave of boredom and sighed. They complained about class coming too soon, but they left for their classes with smiles. While they sat in their classes listening or working, three vans drove into the school front parking lot. The vans open and twenty-four men get out with large duffle bags. They were armed with submachine guns and had masks covering their faces. One of them gets out of the passenger side of the second van. A bulky man, tall, and has a custom mask with an orange color covering the upper left side of his mask. "The cops are going to find us, take the school, as planned we will take the secret escape tunnel. Go." He commands with a calm and demanding voice. They bust through the front door and head towards the office area. Meanwhile Markus and Sasha are sitting with some friends in class. Markus rolls a 20 sided die landing on 6. "6? My unlucky number haha, alright your turn Sasha." He writes the number down as she takes the die. Rolling another 6. "A 6? Guess you can see it as fate we are meant to be together." She giggles as Markus smiles, shaking his head passing it to another. "Alright... Jacob you're up." But before Jacob could roll, Markus heard a creepy raspy voice. "They're coming." Markus turns around with shock and fear. "What!?" Jacob and Sasha looked at each other before he asked "dude you ok?" Markus calms down, looking down before speaking. "Yeah... I'm fine." Jacob puts down the die and goes out of the classroom. "Where are you going?" Sasha asks. "The bathroom, brb heh." Jacob leaves and after a few minutes Markus takes the die before hearing the same voice. "They're here." Markus looks around a little scared. Sasha felt worried, but before she could say anything the announcement came on. "Good students of Highland Park, your school is now under new management, sadly your previous principal and vice principal took a hehe early retirement. So as your new temporary principal, this school will be under lockdown. Anyone who attempts to leave will be expelled. From life. Stay in your classes, continue to work, and you might live." The robbers start entering classrooms, the robbers even find Jacob and toss him into his classroom. Sasha and Markus rush over only so see him bruised and a little bloody. "Damn bastards." Angered and yet scared Markus stares down the masked robber. "What are you looking at brat?" Markus continues to stare before Sasha gets up and pulls Markus back. "Markus, stand down. For now." As the robbers spread out through the school, the police started to search the area. The leader, the orange masked man, walks through the school as a small group of robbers approach. "Hey boss, we found a rich boy with a hot girl. Figured they could be useful for our negotiation." The leader looked at him and behind his mask was an interested smirk. "Really? Show me." Afterwards the man guarding Markus' class received a radio message. "Take the girl and bring the boy." The robber gives a low laugh before saying. "with pleasure alright kiddos, we need some of you. We'll take you..." as he takes Sasha's arm and pulls her. Markus jumps up and pushes him. "Leave her alone, none of us did anything wrong, just do what you need and get out of here!" The robber takes his gun and aims at Markus. "You little shit, I hope you learn respect in the afterlife." He fires his gun, but Sasha gets in the way and drops to the floor bleeding. Markus looks at her scared, feeling a sudden burst of anger and agony. The voice returns with anger and with wraith. "They hurt her, they murdered her. Kill them, destroy them, rip them apart. Kill them master KILL THEM!" Compelled to listen to the voice Markus takes a pencil and rams it into his eye. The robber cries out in pain. "My eye, my fucking eye!" Markus grabs the robber's gun and aims it straight into his other eye. The robber notices and starts to beg for his life. "Please, I didn't mean to- " without any emotion or even flinching, Markus shoots him. His class looks at Markus with a bit of fear, but a few were glad he killed the man. Before anyone could say anything Markus walks out of the classroom and moves down the hall, to be greeted by more robbers. "I heard two gunshots. A kid? Get on your kne-" again before even thinking about it Markus raises the gun and starts to fire at the robbers. The first robber gets shot in the shoulder and neck before falling to the ground, dropping his gun. The second one, surprised, reacted too slowly and got shot in the chest three times. Markus walks down the hallway and into the central area where most of the robbers are. "Why did you come here? If it wasn't for you Sasha would be alive. Sasha, she deserved better. You'll pay, you'll pay." As he continues to say "you'll pay" the voice would copy him both saying "you'll pay". Gunfire echoes through the school. Markus stands behind a concrete wall as he shoots two more times missing both shots. The robbers on the other side pop out with their submachine

"Why am I your Master? How am I even alive!?" Shadow sits on Markus' shoulder. "No idea Master, why did you have to die? Why did you have to live? So many unknowns." Markus looks around seeing quite a few of Shadow's kind. "What are ya, Gremlins? Goblins?" Shadow shows a smile full of his small yet sharp teeth. "Gremlins would be best, though my brothers and I are only to be your servants. Now, with you back alive we have much to do." Shadow vanishes in a cloud of smoke and reappears on the table with a white mask by his feet. The mask itself only has a thick line going down the right eye. Markus walks over to Shadow, calm and collected. "What do you mean? What do we need to do?" Shadow's brother gathers around Markus. "Vengeance master, for those that have been hurt by scum and for yourself, who has lost his old life. The killers who took everything from you, hunt them." As Markus thought of it, he felt like just being a vigilante, but Sasha's voice echoed. "Avenge me, avenge my death." Markus' face turned into a face of hate and pain, taking the mask and putting it on his face. The line on the mask would turn red then blue as it connects to his face. "Find those who work for our good friend Cerberus, bring any info to me, go my servants." The gremlins cheer and laugh as they swarm out of the room.

A small warehouse near an industrial area, a small group of men sat around a table in one of the rooms, a stack of money in the middle and cards in each of their hands. "Ya know, the boss has been visiting each work zone we have in the city. Wonder why." The man next to him draws three cards and flips them face down on the table. "No idea Buck, why don't you go ask him? Bet he'd gladly tell us." Being sarcastic he taps the table, checking. Buck would light a cigar as he looked at his cards, His Light brown hair spiked up with gel. "Like I would dare ask, the last guy to ask lost more than his tongue." Some of the guys shiver. As they talk the sound of a gremlin running is heard. Buck looks over, taking out his cigar. "Anyone hear that?" The dealer laughs "trying to get out of the bet? Nice try." Mischievous laughter is heard and all the men jump out of their chairs and draw their pistols. "Who is there? Get the fuck out and we might let ya live." More laughter is heard as the gremlins mimic the men with a bit higher pitch and raspy voice. "Who is there! Haha, let ya live Ahahaha!" The men feel a sudden cold feeling, terrified. They see movement by a few crates and fire all the rounds they have. After emptying all they have they smile and chuckle. "Bang bang hahaha, banga bang hahaha!" Yellow eyes glow in the dark. The frightened men start to reload their guns, but the lights go out one at a time. The room goes dark and the gremlins rush towards the men as they yell and fire randomly. Within seconds the lights came back on and the only thing remaining was one man. "What the... where did." He hears more laughter and he drops his gun. "WHERE ARE YOU!?" As he is filled with terror and crying the man shakes. "WHAT DO YOU WANT!" as he looks around one of the gremlins says "You." grabbing him by the ankles and dragging him into the dark screaming. The warehouse was once again silent, not even the sounds of a gremlins' laughter was heard. Later in the day in a dark room was Buck, tied up in a chair with gremlins laughing around him. Markus walks in with his mask and a gray trench coat. "Tell me, where is Cerberus? Your boss." Buck, blindfolded, has no idea what will happen to him. "Please man, I didn't do anything, I just guard a warehouse." Markus keeps walking around him, his gremlins laughing. "Where is he? His recent job must have him in hiding." Buck struggles to get out of the bindings. "What job? It has been a month since the last job, just please let me go." Markus stops. "A month? So do you know where he put the money he stole?" Buck, still crying, struggles harder. "I-If I tell you. Will you let me go." Markus smiles behind his mask as he places a hand on his shoulder. "You will be released into the world unharmed. I am a man of my word." Buck stops struggling, hoping to trust Markus. "Ok...ok, he got a job to rob the city bank a-and some big shot CEO ordered it, I don't know who, you gotta believe me!" Markus nods towards the dark. "Just one more thing, where is your boss, where is Cerberus?" Buck clears his throat. "He... he is at a club in the slums, always in the VIP lounge with a couple of girls, that's all I know." Markus walks away and Buck is dragged away in the chair. Markus would enter a room with a couple of guns taken from the warehouse guards. "Shadow!" Within seconds Shadow appears in a cloud behind Markus. "Shadow, did you get anything out of the others, weapons, criminal operations, anything of use?" Shadow would give a chuckle before answering. "Yes master. A few locations with weapon depots. This group is very big on human trafficking and weapon smuggling." Markus smiles as he walks out of an abandoned farmhouse. "They will be runned out of the state, then no one has to deal with gangs and criminals. Before crime ruled this city."

Hours later Buck wakes up in an alley by a dumpster. A note left on his body. It reads "a new life, or a dark past." Buck gets up and walks into the street sighing and going home. Though on the roofs, watching Buck, Shadow sits along with some purple gremlins. "The Master allows him to live, though I can see much use for him. Follow him, kill anyone who can threaten Master's plans." Shadow gives a crooked, evil grin. The purple ones slowly dissipate into mist. The mist floats over the buildings following Buck. After a couple hours Buck reaches his home and unlocks the door. As he enters the purple gremlins pass under him, unknowingly locking himself with two phantoms.

CHAPTER

3

THE GUARD OF HELL

In the fields of the abandoned farmland layed a tractor, sitting in a nice silent day. The sound of gremlin laughter broke the silence as they surrounded the tractor. They cheer like victorious soldiers in war. Shadow and Markus stand staring as a green gremlin stands on top of the tractor taking in the cheers. "Lift high, me lift a big machine!" Markus crosses his arms as he watches. "So the purple ones are able to turn into mist, becoming nearly undetectable, like phantoms. These green ones are able to grow in size and lift things like tractors." The gremlin grows to be about 6 feet tall and has muscles the size of a man's head. It picks up the tractor and throws it almost 2 miles away. Markus looks in shock, though he gives a smirk. "Like a monster. What about the others? What can they do?" Shadow and Markus walk into the barn where the blue and red gremlins are playing around. A few red ones and wrestling with each other while the blue ones are on the ceiling and walls. Shadow points up at the lights as they flicker. "They are able to draw and send electrical surges to any kind of device that uses energy." The blue minions drain the light and then power it up over and over. Markus watches the light. "Shockers, shock the light for power, or blow it and 'shock' the criminals." Shadow gives a chuckle as he looks at the red ones. "They however are able to spread fear and chaos, look into their eyes and your nightmares will arise." Markus rubs the chin of his mask. "Much like demons, I am very impressed, they all have such unique abilities and much promise." He walks out of the barn, pleased, thinking of ways to use each one of them to their potential. He looks towards the city and for a second his eyes and the line on his mask turn red and back to blue.

In the city a small group of men, in nice business suits, were hanging around a dance club in the middle of the night. They were just standing and talking, a few drinks and having plenty of laughs. After a while a car pulls up and the man inside of it signals for them to get in. The men pick up duffle bags and get into the car. They drove for an hour around town and ended up stopping at an abandoned part of the city. They get out and put on masks, the same masks Cerberus and his men had. In their duffle bags they pull out AR-15s and 12 gauge shotguns. As they close into the big abandoned building they were parked by they hear music, DJ type beats ringing through the building, yet silent to the outer world. They open the door and the music blasts out as they walk in. As they walk through the crowd the people are careless, swaying like they are docile and in another world. The four men reach a stairway where a few other men with masks are. They walk up the stairs and enter a room with a skinny man and a scar across his cheek. Two women in his arms giggling and taking pills. "You're so bad Daniel." The man, Daniel, smiles. "Enjoy the dreamers girls, you will need them." He nods his head to another man and he pulls the two girls away into another room. He signals for the new men to come closer. "The hell do you want? Can't you see I am busy gettin business up?" The masked man with a gold stripe on his suit steps up. "The boss is not happy with your current production rate. In his words 'get the production up by twice as much or I'll bite your head off.' He made it clear you are fucking up." Daniel leans forward, angered. "Tell that Cerberus mutt that my dreamers are already drawing in large crowds. If he wants more then open another party club in the area." He points to the other room. "As for those items we already are taking fifteen to twenty girls every two weeks. If you want cops down on us then he can be the first to fall. I've been here longer than that mutt." He smiles before the four men shoot his guards with the shotguns, the two men with ARs point at Daniel. "The boss said you'd make excuses, you're fired." They light him up with every shell and bullet they have. One of the men from before enters shocked and scared, seeing the remains of Daniel. The gold striped man walks up to the other man. "You're in charge, don't upset the boss, else Hell waits for you too." The four men exit laughing. They walk through the crowd, still docile and exit to see a limo. The gold striped man enters the car. "Boss, Daniel did like you said, what now?" The man sitting across from him was Cerberus. "We make everything ours, find others who won't fall in line, make it known the Hounds of Hades own this city." He relaxes, easing back and laughs.

CHAPTER

4

CONTROL EVERYTHING

Police sirens ring through the city. Markus is walking down the street with no mask on, but instead is wearing a hat and hoodie. He turns into an alley with no people, nothing but trash. Before long three men walk out and block his path. "Are you looking for a fix man?" Markus stares at the guys and snaps his fingers. In only a few seconds a few gremlins appear from trash and the roofs tying up the men and gagging them. Their screams and shouts are muffled as they are dragged into a dark room in the nearby building. They struggle and terror is seen in their eyes as the door shuts slowly behind them. Within a few minutes the men were tied to chairs, their backs facing one another. Markus walks in with his trench coat and mask on. "Where are you getting these drugs?" The men struggle as they attempt to break loose. "Fine, you won't tell me." A red Gremlin jumps and stands on Markus' shoulder. "Then he will." The demon stares into one of the men's eyes. As the demon's eyes turned red, like a raging fire, the man that looked into its eyes started yelling in fear. "No... no stay away. STAY AWAY!" he continues to scream, the other two, shocked and confused, start to beg. "Please man, let us go. W-We'll tell you everything! Just don't let that thing near us!" The other man stares at his screaming friend and looks at Markus. "Yeah I swear, anything you want, it's yours, just let us go!" Markus walks around them, still letting the man from before scream his lungs out. "Ok, tell me where your supplier is, where do you get your drugs!?" The demon gremlin's eyes stop glowing and the screaming man passes out. The other two look at Markus and with fewer in their eyes they give up the information. "Yeah, we get it from the docks, every week, Sunday, around midnight we always meet up at an old rusty ship, it never leaves port! Let us go!" Markus could feel they were hiding something. He noticed they didn't say the exact location, nor who they met. Before he could question them more, Shadow appears out of mist on his shoulder. "Master, you can feel it too? Yes the untold truth, they are hiding some information, but in their state... they are useless." Markus looks at the men and can see it, their minds are in a panicked state. "Then we search the whole port from dusk to dawn." Shadow disappears and reappears on the unconscious man and grabs the head of the other. "There is a better way. A way to see into their minds, to know their sins and to know their thoughts. All you need, master, is to place your hand on his forehead." Markus looks at the man and then back at Shadow. "I'm... not sure. There must be another way." Shadow holds the man's head. "There is no other way, master, this man has caused so much pain, so much death, whether he wanted it or not." Markus slowly moves his hand, the man, who is terrified. As his palm is pressed against the man's head, he sees his memories, his childhood to what he is now, what has been done. As Markus takes in every detail within seconds, the man screams in pain. A memory of the docks surfaces and Marlus focuses on it. From the drug dealer's eyes he sees a yellow cargo container with a bird symbol on it. Markus takes his hand off of the man's forehead and, once again, his eyes and the line on his mask changed to red for a couple seconds longer. He shakes his head and the mask and his eyes turn blue. "I know where it is, as for you... your life is horrible, leave this town and find a real job, if I ever come across any of you. You will die." The men nod as the unconscious one starts to wake. "Tell your friend too, release them. We have no time to waste." Markus walks out of the room as phantoms untie the three men and kick them outside. "Dude, these drugs are gonna kill us, so damn scary." Markus stands on the roof above looking towards the shoreline. "So far, why at the docks? It's pretty far from here." *he would continue thinking of reasons why criminals would get the supply from the coast. He thought of if the drug was from other countries. He could feel that it is much more than that. "Perhaps... a cartel has moved into Texas. I need more information before I conclude anything."

Night comes and the monsters that scare children, lurk in the dark to hunt men. The waves crash against the docks and the ships that lay there, dormant. A group of men in suits walk up to the yellow boat that the drug dealers had mentioned. They bang on the hull near the symbol and a secret door opens. As they enter, shadows of gremlins appear on the ground. The door would close and the sound of gremlin laughter would start slowly and get loud. Upon the door opening they scatter and the laughter turns into silence. "Weird, I'm hearing shit." The man shuts the secret door. Behind the door are a couple men with military grade weapons, M16A4 assault rifles, M590 shotguns, and some P90 submachine guns. The guys that came in walked through to another door. Opening it they see crates of both weapons and drugs. "Now we're talking." The men pull out their glocks and place them on a tray and go to sit at the table in the middle of the room. The table has seven seats, four of them taken by the men. After a couple minutes two other men come in and take a seat with the final guy who has a scar on his cheek. "So boys, let's cut the crap and say it, the drugs are bringing in good money, especially with an increase in crime and loss of family. As for guns we are getting them out for good prices." They continue talking as shadows move all around them. The lights start to flicker and die slowly. "Alright very funny boys... now turn them on." Someone moves towards the switch, the sound of his feet would stop before getting near it. His gun drops and hits the floor. "What's going on?" The dark room, once of business, now is the room of death and terror. The men activate the flashlights on their guns. They look around the room, but one by one their guns drop and their bodies are missing. "This is not funny, come on out!" A man walks out of the shadows into the light, but like a puppet his limbs were dead as he moved. Laughter echoed throughout the hull of the ship. The men fire at the body. After seeing the body drop two men investigate it. "He is dead, though not sure how he was mov-" the man falls and gets dragged screaming. "NO, NO WHAT ARE YOU WHA-Agh." His screams stop and laughter echoes once more. A gremlin speaks "Night comes and the damned walk, stars burn the doomed muk. Lifes for the great one, we are never done." Silence enters the room. The armed guards, scared, stay close together. The men at the table take some guns from the floor and watch for any movement. A box drops and thunders as it hits the floor. The sound causes the men to fire in fear at the box. A few gremlins jump on the man behind the rest and bite his neck, ripping it out. The man grabs his throat as he drops dead. The others hear his body drop and turn to shoot at it. The gremlins are gone. "What the fuck is that? A fucking demon!?" A few Gremlins jump onto another man stabbing his eyes, with kitchen knives, before disappearing into the dark. Markus' voice echoes "do you wish to die? My minions hunger for death. If you wish to live, lay your weapons down." The men shake as the guards drop theirs and a few of the men from the table do the same. However the man that has a scar on his face holds his gun. "Think you scare me!? I am Ben fuckin Reigo and I don't scare!" The lights from the guns pop as Darkness shrouds them and a single man screaming is all that's heard. A single light buzzes back on as the room is filled with the bodies that were taken. The remaining men fall to their knees begging for their lives. Markus' voice is heard throughout the ship. "So, are you boys ready to die? Or are you willing to give me what I want and live for another day." They drop to their knees and beg for mercy, while Markus takes in a smell. He walks into the light as his gremlins surround him laughing, his eyes turning red. "You will tell me everything I want to know."

CHAPTER

5

HELL'S FALL

Cerberus sits in a giant room with an eagle view of the city, he stares out of the window onto the city. "So. All of my Lieutenants just vanished, our production is falling and you are telling me that no one knows who is doing it?" A couple men behind him, scared, shake as they try to speak. "We don't know. He...he leaves no signs. Just, bodies and blood." Cerberus turns around and stands up calmly. "Not even a name? How bout a voice, anything. Do you even know what he LOOKS LIKE!?" He slams his fist to the desk in front of him and goes through the desk. The men back away and shake their heads looking down. "No? So a ghost then? The wind? Are we being hunted by demons? That is what they want us to believe. Hunt down every gangbanger who never joined up, torture them to get the information we want, then kill them." The men nod their heads before leaving their boss to his plans. After a while Cerberus gets up and walks to his window looking onto the city. "If we must, we will burn this city just to find him."

Soon after, those under Cerberus would find the other gangs and would begin the slaughter, leaving gangs dead and disorganized. The few that survived these attacks are captured and tortured for any information on Markus, but gaining nothing on him. A warehouse in the outskirts of the city was guarded by Cerberus's gang, the HellHounds. Inside the warehouse, a few men drag someone into an open area and keep him on his knees. They chain his arms to the roof and raise him enough for his knees to get barely off the ground. "Who is the masked man attacking our supplies? He with you?" Says the torturer. The man looks up at him. "He ain't with us, you got the wrong gang, but I do hope he cuts your balls off and feeds you to the dogs." He spits on the torturer. The torturer gets out some jumper cables and sparks them as the man breathes heavily. His screams are heard throughout the warehouse and even outside. Markus stands on the top of the building as the sun starts to set. The men below seem a bit on edge. "I heard the dude attacks only at night, using the darkness." The first HellHound says. The second HellHound laughs. "He can't find us, there's no roads to this place but the dirt roads and we made sure they seem like they lead nowhere. Besides those lanterns are bright enough." For every man there is a lantern that makes them visible. With eight people out in the front patrolling the boring night away, they would soon know nowhere is safe. As the night sends in with screams from inside the warehouse, eight turns to seven as a lantern seems to be out. The two at the gate notice that they are one short. "Hey Jackie, you out there?" The silence gives them shivers. The silence is interrupted by a thud and scream as it gets further away. "It's- It's him!!" The other slowly back to the gate and one by one their lanterns dim and die out. The gremlin laughter is heard as the men cowers in fear. Markus walks up to them holding a gun as he aims at the men. "Surrender... or die." The Hellhounds laugh as they fire at him, filling him with holes as he collapses. The laughter stops as two of the HellHounds walk over to check him, his mask turns from blue to red as he opens his eyes. The two are dragged away as Markus gets up and fires a bullet into one of their heads. The men were shocked to see him come back from the dead. Gremlins rush them, ripping them apart, piece by piece, and eating them as the men scream and pull at the gate begging to be let in. The Hellhounds inside back away from the gate and aim their submachine guns as they listen to the screams turn silent. The silence, deafening, as the fear crawled up their spines, they knew that death was beyond that door. They could not escape it. The gate opens, sliding to the side, as they see the bodies of their dead friends, the eaten corpses lay there with a blue gremlin eating one of the corpses. The HellHounds freak out and either drop their guns and drop to their knees or fire every bullet they have into the pile of eaten corpses. Markus appears behind them. "Surrender, or join your friends." His eyes shine a deep red, his voice even is deeper. The HellHounds, too afraid to reload their guns, drop to their knees and Gremlins rush them, binding them and holding them on the ground as many mumble. "It's a nightmare... a bad dream. A very bad dream." Markus walks to the back room where the torturer and his guards were. The torturer takes a crowbar and swings at Markus as Shadow appears by the torturer's legs and using a knife stabs him in the back of his knee. He falls to the ground holding his leg as the knife hangs in the man's leg. The other two swing at Markus. Markus ducks and grabs one by the throat as a few gremlins long at the other eating him to death. Markus picks the guard up and chokes him, he begs for his life as Markus snaps his neck. Shadow smiles as he vanishes and appears on Markus's shoulder. "Good master, very good. You are ready for the next ability." Shadow says as Markus drops the body. Markus's eyes and mask turn blue again as he feels upset a bit, even scared of himself. "I... I don't know if I am really ready. Or if I want such power." Shadow disappears and reappears in front of Markus. "Master, these are your enemies.

You have many enemies Master. Would you like more allies?" Markus looks at Shadow and then at the corpses around him, the torturer crawling away, bleeding out a slow, painful, death. He then looks to the hurt men and young teenage boys who were next on his chopping block. His eyes and mask turn red again. "You do not know me, to my creatures I am Master. To you I am Kronos, the titan king. If you wish to leave for home and never hurt any innocents through drugs and crime, then you may. However if you want to hurt these men back and become titans yourselves. Join me and put a dagger in that man." Markus opens the doors and his gremlins offer knifes to them, few left without doing the deed, but the rest. They took those knifes and although they hesitated, they plunged their knives into his legs and back. Shadow appears on Markus's shoulder. "Master look at your hands and enjoy your gift." Markus, confused, looks at his palms and sees two symbols. On his left hand is a sword, while on his right hand is a chain. "What are these? What are they for?" Markus looks to Shadow as he walks down his right arm and lands on the floor. "The sword is for those who are loyal servants, your knights. The chain is for slaves, those unworthy of being free, of being human." The men before him look to Markus, waiting for their savior to say something. "Hm… you are free men, if you are to follow me, you will do right by the people. Those loyal will be my agents in the darkness, they will fight in the dark and live in the dark. In order to bring peace and light to the world we must fight in the dark, as a legion. Bend the knee and you will be Titan in this dark world holding the world in your hands and bringing light." They look to him and then to themselves. One man steps up. "We have been brutalized and tortured by evil men. These HellHounds are not good men. I will gladly be part of your legion of darkness. I pledge myself to you Lord Kronos and the Legion of Darkness." He bows to Markus. Markus looks at his left hand with the sword as it glows. Shadow sits on Markus's right shoulder grinning. "He is a true loyal servant. Only the truth will allow you to grant them the right of being your ally." Markus places his left hand to the first man and blue light surrounds the man and as the man stands straight and the sword, branded into his head, glows. Markus brands the sword onto all of their heads as they bend the knee to him. Markus then looks to his right hand and then to the HellHounds he has as prisoners. "Your sins, how sinful are you all?" He waves his right hand in front of them as a red light shines on most of them. The men beg as he brands one of them with his right hand, the sound of a hot iron burning skin echoes through the warehouse as well as the screaming of the man. After the man stops screaming, Markus removes his hand and sees a burnt mark of a chain on his forehead. Markus goes on to the others as he brands them as slaves and Shadow gives an evil smile. Soon they gathered around Markus, the loyal stood tall and Sith pride, but the slaves slouched and coward as the difference between the two was very clear. "My loyal men we shall claim this place of horrors and remake it into a place of hope for the people of Texas. We shall purge our city of Sin and will bring light through our darkness. So go and bring worthy allies. As for our slaves. You will return to your friends and learn of your boss and his operations. You will inform me and will wait for further instructions. The slaves answer "yes master." A loyal man steps up. "What of those who are neither sinful or loyal to you?" He looks to the prisoners they have, the three scared boys laying in the cells. "They will be prisoners until they either swear loyalty or until their masters they serve are dead." Markus says with a calm tone. The slaves and loyals move out.

Weeks later the warehouse was made into a fortress and more men lay within this new fortress. A few slaves use scrap metal to make defenses. A small group of loyals carrying their submachine guns walk towards the warehouse and open it up to many more loyalists. With Markus standing in an upper area watching over them with Shadow. The small group walks up the steps to Markus, one of them with a box. "Lord Kronos, we bring a gift." They move out of the way for the one with the box. One of the men opens the box as they pull out a poorly sewed flag with a black shield behind a white sword pointing downward. "We thought a Lord should have his own banner." Markus gently holds it and looks over it. "It is perfect, the shield of Darkness to bring the sword of Light out." He hands it to Shadow, who vanishes with it and reappears on top of the warehouse raising the banner high. The loyalists look at it with pride as the slaves continue their work. Over the next few months their numbers grew. They had slaves infiltrating and taking more slaves for the Legion of Darkness. When there was a deal going down, loyalists arrived and killed any Hellhound they find, leaving a message for Cerberus. Markus stands on a building with Shadow, a few Gremlins, and a few loyal men as they watch the city. "The gates of Hell were opened, but for too long it stood open. Now Hell is falling to darkness, so light may rise."

CHAPTER

6

THE DEVIL'S HOBBY

An alarm goes off at the break of dawn as someone turns it off and grumbles about waking up. It was Buck who was getting up. He goes to eat some pop tarts, groggy and tired. After he brushes his teeth and goes to watch the news. The entire time he was watched by two phantom gremlins. The news talks about a new gang that is removing crime and making the streets safer. Of course the news also makes a comment about how ruthless they are and that the police should be the only ones doing that. Buck runs his head as he looks out the window to a shining sun breaking through the clouds as it rises. "Ugh. The rent is due and I barely have enough. Doing good is hard. Maybe this new gang of people can help. They seem to be helping people. Or maybe it is a cover up." He gets on some new clothes and puts on his shoes. He walks out and goes down the street with his hands in his pockets. A few guys in yellow shirts, with a bulldog on it, walk behind him. The Phantoms leave and as one leaves and goes another way, the second one keeps tailing the three. Buck turns down an alleyway. He is stopped by a man in a suit with a logo on his shoulder, the logo of a bulldog. There are two men, one of them has his head tilted down like a broken man, but holds a straight, proud, back. They turn to Buck as he looks to see he is surrounded. "Woah. Boys I have no beef with y'all, just let me pass." The suit man smiles. "If you ain't a HellHound, you are not our friend. Who are you with? The Legion of Darkness? Or maybe an FBI agent." They get out knives and the HellHound suit stops smiling as he looks behind Buck. A few guys in black hoodies and shirts stand there with glocks. Before the suit could say anything, the one HellHound with his head tilted takes his knife and stabs the other man in the throat. The Legion boys shoot the two HellHounds behind Buck and the two phantoms appear, jumping onto the suit forcing him to the ground. Buck drops to the ground not wanting to get shot. The Legion boys gag the suit and put a hood over him and help Buck up. "Get home, stay out of trouble dude. This city needs some cleaning." Without a second to spare they drag the suit to a van that pulls up and they get him in as the HellHound slave walks away. Buck stands there surprised and afraid. "What the? What just? They saved me. Why?" He ponders the thought. After a moment he makes a choice. "If they are helping people. I can make a difference with them, maybe help my family too.' He walks only a few steps before a phantom appears in front of him. "Master has been expecting you to join. Master sees much potential in you." Buck, surprised, stays silent, but a small smirk crosses his face.

Buck opens a door to a dark room filled with Gremlin laughter. Buck's fear of the laughter froze him. Markus's voice could be heard "come in young man. It seems you have made up your mind." Buck shallows hard as he slowly walks in. He can tell there are Gremlins all around him, but there are men too. Lights slowly turn on as he walks to the center of the room. The Gremlins have a bit of armor on their shoulders and bodies. The men have Knight like armor on their arms. From their shoulders to their hands are covered by black armor plating. Near the center of the room in front of Buck was a commander pauldron with the arm armor. "What is this?" Markus walks out from behind Buck. "You are a prime candidate for Commander of my Dark Knights. A loyal force that will be my elite, at least that is what my advisor says. There are also some that have seen you take command of the HellHounds and would have made it better. There must be a Blight Commander. Someone willing to do what is needed to win our war against crime." Buck stares at the armor as Markus speaks, walking around him and the armor stand. "However, there are others with promise. There is only one Blight Commander, only one to lead our men to glory. Are you him?" Buck looks down taking a deep breath and standing tall he looks to Markus. "I will prove it. Give me a handful of men, and I will bring the HellHounds to their knees." Markus places his left hand on his forehead as the mark of loyalty is placed on his head. "Will these men do?" The ten men standing in the room step closer. Buck looks around him and nods. "Time to do some good. To change the fate of our city."

Buck and his men gather around a map of Texas and their city. "So boys. Let's think. The HellHounds have three main businesses. Drugs, weapons, and their 'legal' strip clubs." Buck points to the city map where he has circles for strip clubs, Xs for drug warehouses, and the letter G for gun warehouses. One of the men steps up. He had a goatee of brown hair and had a shaved head, his eyes were kind, yet his hands told the stories of his hard labor. "How about we focus on hitting their gun warehouses, stop their weapons from flowing in, stop them from arming more men." Buck smirks "that is smart, tell me your name." The man with a goatee looks at Buck respectfully. "Jones, Jones Halls." Buck points to a gun warehouse. "You are right, but taking each warehouse will take time and more men than we have. No need to lose good men for a couple warehouses. I overheard a slave reporting how all the warehouses are supplied weapons and ammo every few months by an overseas shipment." Buck moves his finger over to the seaport to the East of their city. "Not sure if the drugs and weapons are coming from the same supplier, but we could find out. Stop their shipments, stop their income." They all nod as one of the other men with slicked to the side brown hair and a beard. "Should be quite a feat then. Plus we will be giving the people hope in ending major crime in the state, not just the city. I like this plan." The other men agree. Buck nods. "Yeah, what should we call you?" The man looks up at Buck with a relaxed and friendly look. His brown eyes and black curly hair stand out. "Names Greg McAllister." Buck nods. It is obvious they felt confident in the mission, a bond of brotherhood grew among them.

A cargo ship, with a paint job of Posiedon on the side, sails towards Texas. The Caribbean sea crashes against the ship in the dead of night. A few men watch over the boat as they watch the cargo containers and mingle with each other, unaware of what approaches. A speed boat races towards it, however they cut the engines a couple miles in front of it and wait for the large ship to pass by. A hook was tossed onto an emergency ladder and, as quietly as possible, moved the boat close enough to get some men aboard. The men wore black garbs, ones that look like the members of the Legion of Darkness. Silence befalls the cargo ship as they make their way through the crew of the ship, killing them quietly. Effectively eliminating all problems they see in their way of a flawless victory. In moments every guard in the cargo area is gone, only blood and water litter the deck. The men regroup at the bridge of the cargo ship and breach silently, killing all the men in the command deck. Buck walks up to the captain of the ship from behind. He taps his shoulder. As the captain turns to see his killer, Buck thrusts a knife into his throat. The shock and surprise on the captain's face made Buck feel bad. "If you wanted to live. Should have never helped bad men." Buck stared at him as he died. He sighs and walks to the controls and stops the boat as the outside team fires a flare into the air. Buck walks out as a few more boats roll up as men throw hooks onto the boat and climb up and start taking the crew captive, nearly all of the crew, including the captain, was marked with the HellHound tattoo of a Bulldog on fire. The ones who didn't have it were young men. Buck made a proposition, they could join them and become better men for it. They could stop the wrongdoings of the men they were with. Some of them were interested. Those who didn't want to join were given a boat and would be left alone. Buck takes a few men and starts opening containers seeing hundreds of crates of weapons, drugs, and a few crates had women inside them with chains around their necks. Bruises all over their bodies and some seem like they haven't eaten in days. Buck is appalled and yells with anger and a bit of sadness. "Get some food and bolt cutters now!" After freeing many, the last container with enslaved women was opened as they would bring in some food and bolt cutters. The women all feared them, thinking it a trap or worse. "Worry not ladies, the Legion of Darkness has presented you with a spark of hope. It is yours to light aflame."

They were still fearful, the men of the Legion would cut their chains and allow them to exit the container.

After a couple hours of helping the women who were imprisoned in their own dark and horrid cells, Buck would speak to one of them. "I am Buck, Knight of the Legion of Darkness." One of the women gets up, wrapped with a gray blanket and beaten. Her hair was long and as black as the dead of night, her eyes were a story of pain and suffering. "We are not certain whether to throw you in with our captors as Hungry men, or to consider you our heroes." She gives them an icy glare. The knights would be cautious, slowly bringing food and clothes to the scared and terrified women. The Deafening silence as the woman stares at the men, as the men watch the women, their hearts heavy with sorrow. The Silence interrupted by only the sounds of waves crashing into the hull of the cargo ship. Buck steps up and breaks the silence glares. "We are here to set you free, nothing else. We will do our best to send you back to your homes."

After an hour the cargo ship would dock with the port in Texas. Police would arrive to take the women and care for them. The knights had disappeared, not a trace of them, nor the dead crew.

CHAPTER

7

DARKEST CORNERS

Whispers grow in the city, in the state of Texas. Ever since the women freed on that cargo ship, people talked about the vigilanties. "I heard about some men rescuing those women." "Did you hear about those drug dealers? Disappeared without a trace." "Some monster killed those men at that Warehouse a week ago." The Talk of the underworld was almost always about the Legion of Darkness. Drug dealers would begin disappearing. Businesses that made deals with the HellHounds suddenly went bankrupt. The Criminals of the city would soon be hunted, one by one. Members of the Legion would gather in number. The HellHounds and any other criminals would hear whispers of the Legion, of how they silence their operations. The People and media would know nothing but rumors and murmurs.

Meanwhile the Police would be motivated to stop this gang war, as they believe it is. A Police Woman and man would be in a room with pictures of what seems to be HellHound members and Legion of Darkness members. The woman had dirty blond curly hair and brown eyes. On her chest was a tag: Officer Thornvel. The man had short brown hair, along with brown eyes, combined with a stubble of hair on his face. On his chest was a tag: Officer Gordon. They had been gathering all they could on what the Legion and HellHounds have been doing. "How did such a new gang become such a challenge? I have never heard of these guys before. And how are they finding the HellHounds and their illegal operations?" Thornvel said with a focused stare at the pictures. "No idea, but they have been dropping their operations like flies. They seem to be directed at the HellHounds. If we had to choose who to take down first,

I would say the Legion guys. They've been raising their body count." Gordon said with a stern look. They would look at all the pictures and information they have. "There is nothing on operations." Thornvel said, searching the documents. "Nothing at all. It is like they are only killers. They could be illegals that crossed the border. But that can't be right, they would have set up operations and caused a rise in drugs." "Perhaps they are a mercenary group? Either way I say we should turn our focus onto the Legion boys. They've grown too big in such a small time." Thornvel and Gordon nod in agreement, heading out of the station.

At the farm, Markus was walking down to the barn where enslaved men were digging and building underground in the barn. There would also be a line of eight men on their knees and binded with rope on the side. Shadow would appear on Markus's shoulder. "Master, We should work our slaves harder. The underground base plan will be slow and unfinished if we don't." "Quiet Shadow, as much as these enslaved men are horrible and have had terrible actions, they don't deserve to suffer more than they already have." Shadow would bow his head in acceptance. "Yes Master, as you wish." Shadow would vanish in his dark mist once more as Markus would enslave three of the eight. "These five are neither worthy nor guilty. Toss them into the pit." The men would pick up the five as they released the other three. One of the men would approach Markus. "Lord, Shouldn't we give those guys to the Police?" Markus turns to him. "No, we must be careful with the HellHounds, if they have their hands in some crooked cops or judges, then they would just release their own men. Then more deaths would come from this 'gang' war. If food is an issue then I will have some of the guilty start harvesting and planting crops." Markus said as he would pat the man on the shoulder. "Makes sense, though Food will be a problem in the near future. Funds will start to disappear. Having a workforce team is working for now, but we can only do so much with so many of us." "I understand, We should hit another HellHound operation and sell their weapons to a gun store, or maybe a Texas militia group." The man nods before returning to work. Markus would look at the farmland and would raise his enslavement hand up. "Plant crops, and harvest. Do my bidding."

In the city Thornvel and Gordon would be riding in their police car. Gordon would be driving as Thornvel would watch out for any crime or strange activity. She would notice a few eyes following their car. "This place is giving me chills up my spine. Feels like they are all glaring at us." "Yeah, Which gang do you think they are? Legion or HellHound." "We won't know just from their stares, pull over. Maybe we can find something out." They pull over to the curb. Getting out they could already feel the tension, the anger. Men in suits would watch the police, hiding behind sunglasses and their phones. Thornvel and Gordon would walk around looking for any symbols and signs. The neighborhood was a middle class area, though it had some areas of trash. They walk to a few of the people in the area, while most show a hint of fear or discomfort, some would talk with the officers. "Hello sir, mind telling us if you have seen any activity that is Gang based?" "Dog, I don't know a damn thing." The Man walks to his porch and sits. Officer Gordon would look to Thornvel before continuing his questions. "Sir, there have been reports of criminal activity in the area. Can you tell me if there has been any sign of the Legion gang?" The man on the porch would Sit back. "I haven't seen anything, other than all this trash. Man, where are all the dump trucks? We haven't had garbage pick up for 3 weeks." They look at each other and then the garbage. They would have a shamed and saddened heart as they see the community filthy. Thornvel would walk over to the man. "We can get a garbage truck over as soon as possible, but the mayor deemed it too dangerous with all the disappearances and deaths." The man sighs and looks around. "Listen, I don't know anything. Most of what happens is in the dead of night, when crime is at the highest. But you heard nothing from me." The man goes back into his house. Gordon and Thornvel would go back to their car and drive away. They would be watched by the men in suits. As they drive away one of the suits would call someone. "Boss, the cops are starting to take interest in our shit." Cerberus's voice would speak through the phone. "Expected. They will be dealt with one way or another."

Night would come within no time as the two officers would slowly roll down the streets watching with determination. Their eyes watching the darkest corners of the streets. The deepest depths of the alleys. With only the dim light of the moon and a few scattered street lights. "Even these Streets give me the creeps. We have nothing on whether there is gonna be any crime tonight." "Even so, there is no other way to figure out where they are coming from. It sucks to do a case with no info." Thornvel sighs as she looks outside towards the alley that would come up as they drive down. She sees a man standing by the corner as he watches them. He stands there in black, her eyes barely picking him out of the darkness. "Well if the Legion of Darkness lives up to their name, I think we got them." They stop their car and slide over to the sidewalk as they get out pulling out their flashlights. The man in dark clothing would walk into the dark alley, already the Officers got a bad feeling.Gordon would take a deep breath and walk forward. "Hello? Police." Walking down the alley, red eyes would watch them from the darkness itself. They felt uneasy. Fear would enter their hearts with each step forward, soon they would barely move as they heard laughter. The same laughter of the gremlins. The Officers would start to sweat bullets as their eyes dart around the alley. Too scared to even make a single movement. Soon enough their fear vanished as men in suits walked into the alley. "So Officers, what brings you all here? In such a dark alley?" Thornvel would be shaking as she turned to see the men. "Um, we were. We were searching the area for criminals. The area has a lot of... crime." Before she finished she realized they were surrounded by men in suits. "Well well well, you found us. Now it is time to rid ourselves of dogs that have broken the chain." the man pulls out a glock 18 from his suit and points it at them. Gordon and Thornvel would still be petrified, unable to react in time. The man smirks as he goes to squeeze the trigger. Suddenly one of the men drops and is dragged away screaming. Everyone in the alley is shocked, paralyzed from the sudden burst of fear. Laughter is heard from every direction. The man who drew his gun would suddenly be pulled up from nowhere screaming as he flew up to the roof. After only a few seconds his screams would go completely silent. The last two men in suits would attempt to run away only to be heard screaming, then complete silence. Gordon would be the only man able to move after the horror they had just witnessed ended. He takes Thornvel's hand and pulls her back to their car where they rush in and drive away in a panic. "What the Hell happened!?" Gordon yelled, breathing heavily. "I-I-I have no idea. It all happened so fast. I could barely move." They drove a few miles away from the area, but no matter how far they drove, that moment remained. Later, at the crack of dawn, a police unit would investigate the area along with Thornvel and Gordon. They find two of the bodies, both stabbed once, directly to the heart. The police would be confused to one point as the men looked as if they were horrified beyond measure. Gordon looks around for another body. "There were four of them, where is the other's body? We should have four bodies." Hours of searching lead to no bodies, yet on the roof, blood covered a large area. Markus would stand on a nearby roof watching them. "The police have finally taken action. I should find some willing to join us." Shadow would crawl up to his shoulder as he smirks a twisted grin. "Or find the corrupt ones and punish them." Markus would hold his chin in his hand as he thinks. "That might be the only way to do this as of now. We will focus on the Crime network first." Thronvel would look around and out of the corner of her eye she saw Markus standing on the roof. She would stare at him, but after blinking he would vanish. Shaking her head, she would believe she was seeing things. She felt what she saw was real, but her mind couldn't put together how he could vanish in a blink.

Back at the station an Officer gets a call. "Hello? Yeah. Gordon and Thornvel took that. No problem. Same fee as before. It is a pleasure boss." The Officer would hang up as he gave a crooked grin. His hazel eyes would have a sense of greed within them. His bald head would shine in the sun as he drank with a few other cops.

CHAPTER

8

MISTRESS OF SHADOWS

The City was always known for their dangerous nights, yet there was one area that was always partying. Most refer to it as the Party zone. A large club called "Kings of Pleasure" would be in the center of the party zone. Young men, gangsters, and every criminal or youngster would know this place and come to party. Inside the club there are three areas. The party area, VIP area, and area for their boss. The party area would have drugs, alcohol, dancers, and plenty of music. The VIP area, on the other side, would have private rooms where ladies would chat with men and other women and indulge in their fantasies. Finally in the final area, the upper level could see all of the rooms below and had a large room where a woman sat on a large purple couch. A man in a business suit would be kissing her feet as she looked down at him bored. "Ugh, your groveling bores me. Your time is up." "no please my lady, I will do anything." She calls some guards over with the wave of her hand and they drag the man out through a back door. "Such a boring man, why do they all grovel? They take the fun out of pleasure." One of her guards would walk in. "ma'am some big shot gangster wants to see you." She looks at him still bored. "Fine, better be worth my time." The guard would bring in Cerberus, in his business suit. He walks in as if he owned the club. As he walks up to the lady he bows like a gentleman. "Lady Reyes Tonka. I see your business is still booming. Even my own boys have become drawn to this place." She grew bored as she looked away, towards a shield and two swords mounted on her wall. "Have I offended you in some way?" "You bore me, I have no care about your Hellhounds or any of the gangs that continue to do their little fights." Cerberus would look at her with a bit of anger.

"Here I thought we could Discuss business. Your business is in danger of Police investigation." She glares at him and stands up. "I know the HellHounds own the Cops, but threatening me will not go well. Many Of our clients are businessmen and men of the law. You take one step in here with that idea and you and your boys will be banned." Cerberus would bow once more. "Very well, if that is what the Queen of the night wishes." He walks out of the building and towards his limo. Before getting in he looks back and scoffs at the club.

Weeks later Markus would be walking streets maskless, yet wearing the rest of his gear. The voice of Shadow would be heard in his head. "Master, your skill is command, making the plans, not action." "I can not expect my own men to follow me if I do nothing myself. If I must, I will show them my strength. With iron and death." Markus would come across some men in suits harassing a woman in a purple dress. "Listen lady, your boss had her chance. Either join us now, or You'll join the Bitch and the others." Markus would put his mask on as the Blue line and eyes would glow. He walks over to them and taps one on the shoulder. They turn around confused and surprised. "HellHounds? What do HellHounds want with a girl, back off idiot, HellHound business. Get out of here before you get hurt." Markus smirks under his mask as he takes his pistol and shoots one of them through the knee and the other in the face as he turns in shock. The girl in the purple dress would run towards the corner of the street as a few other people ran away. "Not very nice now are you?" The man yellings about his knee would breathe as he turned to Markus with an angry and cocky grin. "Oh you are screwed, When my boys hear you killed one of us they will hunt you down." "Oh? Think they will be the first to catch me? I am the leader of the... Legion." The grin and anger turn to a sudden state of fear. "I-I'm sorry. We don't need to do this, I'll tell you everything. Our boss wants the club downtown. So much so that he has already started to get some boys to take it in a few days. We-we were sent out to take some of the girls with us willingly or not to Make sure the takeover will work without damaging the good!" Talking rapidly the man would be in a state of panic. Markus would take his gun and shoot a couple bullets into the man. He then walks down the street. Shadow's voice would return. "A raid we can interfere with and confront their boss. Revenge is ever more closer." "Indeed, get some boys together. We have some Plans to make." Markus would return to the farm as he makes plans to take the Club from the HellHounds and weaken the HellHounds.

While the plans for the Kings of Pleasure are being made in the dark, Reyes Tonka would be standing in her palace, watching her club party. A black Wolf would walk into her room as she turned, she went over to the wolf and played with his face. "Waffles! Oh who's a good boy!? You are, yes you are!" She plays with her wolf, Waffles, until a guard walks in. Her smile and joy would disappear with the sight of the guard. "What is it? Can't you see I am with my pet?" "Yes ma'am, but one of your girls has reported HellHounds getting handsy in public. From the sound of what the men said they seem to have targeted the club." Reyes walks to her couch where Waffles lays on the couch with her placing his head in her lap. "So how did she get away from them? One of our guards spotted this?" "Um… no ma'am. She said a man in a mask and black trench coat came up and shot the men. She didn't hear what he said to them after. He walked away after offing the last guy." She pets Waffles as she thinks. Dismissing the guard she would pounder. Later that night she would have all her girls stay at the club and send her guards to get them dinner. She would hire some extra guards for her club. Vigilant day and night for when the HellHounds would make their move.

Finally, After days of planning and waiting. One night while the guests party and the guards watch. Midnight stuck as HellHound cars and trucks roll up to the club and begin to push people out of the way. The bouncer would stop them, only to be met with a bullet in the skull. The people outside start to panic and flee. While inside the music would barely drown out the sound of the gunshot. Though panic would slowly envelop the rest of the club as people tried to get out of the soon to be gunfight. The HellHounds and the guards would pull out pistols and would start shooting at each other. Both sides would kill each other. Bullets would fly through the club as people hide or run around finding a way out or a place to lay low. The guards would flip tables and use the DJ stereo as cover. The music would still be going as the club is riddled with bullet holes. A group of HellHounds would make their way to the upper floor to take out Reyes. As they gun down anyone in their way towards Reyes's "Throne room". As they enter the first man up front is jumped by Waffles. Tearing his throat out as two other guards gun down the others with shotguns. Waffles drags the body back to Reyes who crouches and pets him. "Oh who's a good boy, yes you are! My bloody Waffles!" She stops petting him as she watches the HellHounds do their best to enter her room. After seven HellHounds were torn apart by shotguns, they stopped rushing. "It is over Reyes, your club is ours!" "You will take this over my dead body. Waffles won't let that. Isn't that right my perfect boy!" After a few shots go through the door, a flash bang rolls in blinding her two guards. The HellHounds roll in and kill her guards, filling them with holes. They walk into her room, four in all. "You are ours to play with Miss Tonka." She glares at them with a look of disgust. "I am to be killed by pathetic worms? Attempt to have your way and my Waffles will rip you all apart." The men would walk slowly up as they grin. Before anything could happen, Markus and a few Dark Knights would fly through the window and gun down the startled HellHounds. Within seconds the intruders were put down without worry. Markus looks around and sees Reyes surprised with her wolf. Markus walks over and pets Waffles. "Are you two alright? The Scum are dead. Do not worry." Reyes looks at him puzzled. "What are you doing?" Markus gets up and takes his pistol and moves towards his men. "Taking care of trash." His eyes and the line on his mask turn red. Reyes would be a bit impressed as she goes to sit in her chair and watch Markus. Markus and his knights would walk through the halls Coming across a few HellHounds trying to pin some hostages and tie them up. The Knights would place their AR-15 carbine rifles against their heads and execute them. Markus would use his Gremlins to hunt down stragglers as well. The upper floors would be filled with corpses and blood. Markus walks down to the lower level. One of the HellHounds would knock his pistol out of his hands, yet Markus would elbow him in the chest and draw his second pistol shooting him 3 times in the chest. He then makes his way to the other HellHounds. His Knights behind him as they gun down any HellHound who peeked their head out. The night of blood was over within the hour. One of the Hellhounds is shot in the leg as he attempts to leave the club. Yelling in pain as he tries to crawl away. Markus walks towards him and with his crimson red eyes glowing bright behind his mask he would aim his pistol down at him. The man turned and began to beg. "Please, I will leave, I'll tell Cerberus that-" His last words were that of fear as Markus would pull the trigger. His blues eyes return as he begins to feel fear for his own actions. "We left no survivors." He takes a deep breath as he looks to his men. The very Knights who he trusted, celebrated the killings and the carnage they had created. "We did it, we took on a Large HellHound op and came out without loss!" Markus knew that there would be a few dead knights, but the fact the guards of the club had held their own so well gave them the chance to wipe out the HellHounds Assault. Markus would check on Reyes's personal guards even having his Knights stop celebrating to aid them. Markus goes to one of the few HellHound survivors and would pick him up slamming him to the wall. "What was the goal here? Pure chaos?" The man would cough a bit as he groaned in pain. "Screw you, who do you think ya are?" Markus would pull him from the wall only to slam him back into it, his mask's line and eyes turning red. "I am Kronos, a Titan who will consume your life." The wounded gangster laughs before Markus puts him in the ground placing his boot on his throat. Reyes walks down stairs speaking up. "Wait Kronos, If you want information. I can handle that." She walks over to Markus seductively. Markus would scoff and lift his boot. The Gangster coughs and looks over to Reyes as she treats the man warmly. "Poor man, you are on the wrong side of this fight. I must say your bravery makes me feel things. Perhaps if you joined me and tell me what you know-" She would whisper to him before picking her head up. The Gangster gulps as a smirk replaces his painful face. "Alright. Cerberus wants to take the rest of the city, any illegal or legal place not under his control would soon follow... to rout the Legion of Darkness and their annoyance." Reyes holds the man's head softly "Then embrace me." She pulls him in close before twisting his head and killing the man. Her smile stays as she stands up. Markus watched her, unphased as he stood over the body. "Thank you for the info miss." His eyes turn blue again as Reyes would look to Markus. "Reyes Tonka. And who are you, my knight from the darkness." Markus would walk away before saying "Kronos to you, prove worthy and I might tell you my old name." Reyes would smile and take interest in him. "Oh? Sounds like I am going to have to tag along." She would soon follow Markus as dawn came, the Club was secured. Though everyone in the city would soon know that their city is in for a long ride.

CHAPTER

9

THE WRONG ARM OF LAW

While Police had arrived late to the Club of Kings, they would shut down the club and make it an active crime scene. Though they could not keep it shut for long. While there were clear signs of fighting and multiple reports, the bodies were gone, the blood floors were clean, and the club seemed to be under construction to hide the bullet holes. While the investigation only lasted a few days, Gordon and Thornvel would take the case into their own hands.

At the Police station Gordon and Thornvel would be in the captain's office. Thornvel's voice could be heard outside the office. "Please captain, give us the go. We can find out how to take these scumbags down." The Captain was a calm man with dark skin and a gray beard and slicked back hair. "As much as that would be great, we have no warrant and no reason. The Club is 'under construction' and most of the noise complaints are not enough. No one is willing to tell what happened either." Gordon would be in the corner of the office looking out the window at the city. "There has to be someone right captain?" "yeah there will be, I know it." Thornvel would jump in as she is very passionate about taking down the Criminals who destroy their city. The captain would take a sip of his coffee as he sighs and turns to his computer. Thornvel would lean in. "Captain Harklight we can do this." The Captain sighs again, obviously not happy about the idea. "Fine, but if anything goes wrong you are done. The case will be closed and you two will not proceed any further." Thornvel nods. "We will get it done. Come on Gordon." They walk out of the office and towards their police car. "Well the Captain seems like this is a bad idea, and has a short leash on us." "Gordon, don't worry, we can do it. You want to back out now?" Gordon shakes his head as he gets into the driver seat. "No, though we will need to tread carefully. There is something wrong with these gangs." Thornvel joins her partner. They would drive off to the Club eager, yet cautious. They would arrive at the club eager to get to work, until they notice a few Officers just relaxing at the club. Gordon would be confused as to why other Officers were here. "Hey, what are you two doing?" The other officers turn to them, and keeping their relaxed tone, speaking confidently "Hey sarge, we are just checking out the place. For a simple club, sure looks like a special place." Thornvel walks over with a serious face. "Well this is our case. Head back to the station." They look at each other and then back at Gordon and Thornvel as they nod "sure you got it." They walk away and get into their own police cruiser driving away as one of them seems to be calling someone. "You get a bad feeling from that?" Thornvel says watching them drive away. She would be suspicious as the club began to give them both chills. "Yeah, just like the alley. We should be careful, extremely careful." After a moment of calming their nerves they walk into the club and begin asking the working girls and customers if they were in the club during the night of the firefight. Yet everyone would deny a firefight or even deny the deaths of any co-workers. A few customers would tell them they were drunk or were enjoying the party too much to notice. Gordon would cross one of the working girls cleaning up a VIP area. "Hello miss. I am Officer Gordon. Mind telling me what happened a few nights ago when the club decided to remake the main area?" The girl has a spanish accent as she looks at the officer annoyed. "Nada, go bother someone else. I gotta get this area cleaned for any other guests." "Mind if I ask why the Club is still taking on VIPs or doing small parties still?" "Gotta keep making money, not all of us live on fat checks from the government." Gordon would sigh as he looked around. He would see a bullet hole by a couch in the VIP area. Walking over before a bouncer steps before him. "You VIP?" "No I am a-" "Then get out. New VIP here." The girl would walk past the bouncer and go upstairs. Gordon would stand his ground. "This is a police investigation, I can arrest you for interfering, or tampering with evidence." The two argue for a bit as tensions between Gordon and the bouncer get close to physical as Reyes walks down. "Officer, is there a problem?" Reyes said in an innocent tone and being a bit seductive. Gordon would see her and like many others fell for her innocent attitude. "Uh, your Bouncer is just interfering with Police work." Reyes would look confused as she speaks to her bouncer. "Let the good officer do his job Jimmie." Her bouncer nods and walks away. Gordon would sigh with relief that it didn't get out of hand. "Thank you ma'am. Officer Gordon." Reyes giggles and walks over to lightly shake his hand. "Nice to meet you handsome. I am Reyes Tonka, I own this Club. Can I help in any way?" She would get close and playing with his head flawlessly as her innocent attitude was very convincing. Gordon would begin to stumble on his words as stands there letting her get closer. "Well I um. If you can let me go around checking the club I can finish this investigation." Reyes would nod as she looked up at him with a smile. Thornvel walks over after being annoyed at the fact the workers and customers refuse to say a thing. "Gordon! What the hell are you doing!?" Gordon snaps out of it as he looks at Thronvel. "Nothing! I was trying to do my job." "By getting a good time with- you know what, you can do your thing I don't wanna know. But we are active." Reyes cuts in and backs away. "Sorry officer, I was just curious if you two needed help." Thornvel looks at Reyes with annoyance as she shakes her head in disappointment. "Right... tell us what happened during the night of the firefight or construction night." Reyes would tell them the same as all the others but adds that the previous Owner had bad taste. She would give a hint as she looked around nervously, acting as if she was worried someone would hear. She then whispers. "I will say everything in my office, walk in through the back door." She would walk away heading up stairs.

Gordon and Thornvel would be confused and do as she said. They would leave the club and drive to the back area which was left open for them. They would feel the shock and terror they once felt in the alley once more. The laughter echoing in their minds as they look at the open door. They pull themselves together, getting a grip on their fear and brave the storm of terror that played before them. As they step into the doorway their terror and fear lifted as the echo laughter vanished. Thornvel would be shaking as she leans against the wall as Gordon would be sweating a bit much. "You ok down there?" Reyes says as she looks down at them like a curious kid would. "We are fine, just the heat." Gordon answers and he wipes his forehead and walks up the stairs with Thornvel following close. Both regaining their strength as they enter a small office with a desk and 3 chairs, not the same office that Reyes ruled from.

"Now that we have some privacy I can tell you what the others fear." Thronvel raises an eyebrow as she takes out her notepad. Reyes would sit in her chair slowly as she shakes. "That night, a few gangbangers with the words HellHounds on their shoulder walked in. They were unhappy with some of my girls, the poor girls. They shot up the place after being refused. Killed a few of my girls, they didn't deserve it. They broke into my office and took some of my girls and threatened to kill them if we didn't be quiet." She begins to cry as Gordon comforts her, even Thornvel would be tricked by her performance. "What about this Legion of Darkness? Were they there?" Thornvel asked curious about this secret gang. "There was a fight between some other gang with them but it was short. In order to keep my girls safe I put up the construction idea and told everyone to be quiet and that we can bring their friends back if we are quiet." She wipes her tears away as she takes a tissue from her desk and cleans her eyes. Gordon and Thornvel would watch her, Gordon being less observant than Thornvel. However neither of them would see any lies in her body movement. "Thank you Miss Tonka, we will get them back." Reyes hugs Gordon, thanking him over and over. Moments after she calms down they take their leave. Reyes would smile innocently at them as they leave. Once gone her innocent smile turns to an evil grin. "I am so good." Markus walked out of the shadows with a grin himself. "You are pretty skilled. Keep that up and keep the police focused on the HellHounds. Good officers. Perhaps one day they will see the use of the Legion." "Oh please my Lord, you are too kind. The Officers are not gonna let you go even if your cause is righteous. They follow a broken system." Reyes says as she looks at him with a convincing worried face. "If they were to know you they would arrest or kill you just because they don't understand. They are bound to the system and will destroy you and your goals if they get you." Markus would glare at her coldly. Reyes would be surprised. "That system may be broken but it can be repaired. We just must punish the criminals who work within it. You could be one of them." He turns and walks up stairs as Reyes smiles. She would watch him walk up. "So cold, so bad. I will unlock the evil I you darling and we can rule." She would say to herself before walking up after. Shadow would be on the ceiling grinning, liking this Reyes and would turn to mist.

CHAPTER

10

WAR OF THE SOUL

Since the Club Massacre, agents of the Legion would grow across the city and even into other towns and cities. With gangs and criminals wary, police and officials became more outspoken. The law would begin to reinforce and even the crooked cops would slowly be cornered and taken down. The streets became filled with the working class and more outgoing teens. Among these people are secret Legion members, from the enslaved who would be placed into the HellHounds or the Loyal agents spreading word of their crusade against crime. Though a familiar face would walk the streets, exploring, DJ. Markus's best friend.

DJ was walking down the street often stopping at stores to get some work. Only recently graduated from school, he wanted to begin his career. He made his way down an alleyway and noticed a big red and yellow hummer behind a condemned building. "Woah, nice ride. A bit big, but nice." He would get closer to it checking it out as he notices the HellHounds tag on the back. "Oh shit." As soon as those words left his mouth he heard a click as the hammer of a glock was pulled down locking. DJ would begin to panic a bit as he slowly raises his hands. "You just had a bad day huh? Nice truck, but wrong people." The man behind DJ says before shoving him into the condemned building. A few extra unlucky people were inside, tied up and terrified. "What the-" DJ is shoved once more as he is put on his knees and hands. The sound of heavy footsteps came closer. The small room had eight other people and five members of the HellHounds locked and loaded with Mac-10s and M4 military rifles. After one of the doors opens, Cerberus walks in, eyeing the hostages. "Get them ready. We have a heist to finish." They are given the clothing of the HellHounds. Tape placed on their mouth and hidden with bandanas, their eyes covered by shades. Even given cardboard replicas of the Mac-10s. "Drop the guns and we drop you. Understood." They all nod as they are pulled into 3 separate vans. One of the HellHounds would be a bit more slouched and would make a quick call away from the others.

After a few minutes driving around they arrive at the biggest bank in the city. The HellHounds and false HellHounds get out and move into the bank and begin their robbery. Though on a building nearby Markus stood, his eyes and mask line was red with fury. "Cerberus. I found you. I will make you pay." He pulls out two glocks and moves across the rooftops to reach the Bank unnoticed. "Find who is my enemy and who was dragged into this war. Unmask the hostages." Gremlins laugh as a few Phantom Gremlins turn to mist and enter the bank searching all of them and leaving a small red mist that only Markus could see. Markus enters the bank quietly as the HellHounds collect money and break into the vault. Markus would take out a knife and grabs one of the HellHounds, cutting his throat and gaining the attention of the crew. Markus stares them down with a fiery red glare. "Where is Cerberus?" The HellHounds fire at Marksus who takes cover behind a pillar. Once everyone emptied their clip into the pillar the hostages in HellHound clothes are revealed as their masks and shades are ripped off their faces. The sudden surprise to the hostages causes them to fall or drop their cardboard guns. The sudden dropping of everything caused the attention of the HellHounds. Turning and giving Markus the chance to step out and use his pistols shooting at the other two HellHounds in the main room. Shooting the first in the leg and then head as Markus walks by. Then placing a few rounds in the other one's chest. The hostages flee the main room. Markus would turn to go to the vault and sees one more hostage being held at gunpoint. It was DJ. At the sight of his friend Markus stops dead in his tracks and his eyes and mask turn blue. "Dany?" Markus speaks to himself. The man holding DJ would back up to the vault. "Back off! Or I will end this bastard!" Markus would stand there glaring at the man as he worried for DJ. "Take the man's gun. Do not risk DJ." He whispers as the man backs up. A Phantom Gremlin would solidify and grab the gun pulling the man away and releasing DJ who dives to the floor. Markus's red eyes return as he picks his pistols up and gun down the man with every bullet he has loaded. Markus regains his blue and walks over to DJ. "You ok sir?" "Yeah bro. Thanks man." Markus nods and walks into the vault as the last HellHound stood grabbing all the money he could. "Where is Cerberus?" He freaks out and pulls his pistol. Before he could aim it at Markus, Shadow grabs his arm as gremlins seal the vault. The light slowly dimmed. "Tell me where he is. What his plan is. And any other operations you have." The vault was sealed and the light went out as many yellow eyes glowed around him with laughter. Outside the vault not a single sound left it. It would be only 2 minutes before police arrive and investigate. They would open the vault only to see the vault had all the money, and a man hanging from his feet. There was no sign of a way to escape. Hours later they see the ceiling has been cut into allowing a person to fit into, but would require two people to get up to it. Markus had used this to escape after getting what he wanted.

DJ would be on his way home as he sighs and is displeased with his cowardice. "I can't believe I let that happen…" he would arrive at his apartment and walk into his home only to be greeted by Markus, with his mask on. "Hello good sir." "What the hell are you doing here!?" Markus would be distorting his voice enough to be unknown to DJ. "You must be angry at those scum. They took you hostage and I can tell they must have hurt you before. Why not join us and end their terror." DJ sits in a dinner chair and relaxes a bit. "To be honest. I don't wanna fight them. They are criminals and I am all for them being arrested and judged by the people. Yet your crew is just as dangerous as them. Can you assure your Legion won't end up like them." "We will never do what they do. We are the people who are tired of crime going unchecked. And many agree." Markus walks to the window looking out at the city. The apartment is on the third floor of the building. "You say that now man. But Power has the chance to corrupt. Think you can maintain that corruption?" Markus remains silent as he holds his head as he gets a spike of pain. "I…I can, I can maintain the power." DJ looks at this stranger with disbelief before getting back up and getting some leftovers from his fridge. "If you are better in the end then we both know you can do this without anger and hateful people. I have to go meet a friend soon. Good luck." Markus would step out of his window and climb to the roof.

Back at the farm the Legion's HQ had grown. The barn became a fortified barracks for the slaves with a wall around the entire farm and it's land. The house would have a few members living in it acting like farmers. But they made an underground base. Though there is only dirt and wood planks here and there. Markus would be sleeping in the master bedroom of the farm house. While the world was calm his mind was not. Markus would be standing in a white room with two statues. To his right the statue would be a Knight with a sword. The sword has the words "Justice, order, peace" on the blade. To his left was another knight with a shield. On the shield were the words "Protector, guardian, freedom". Markus would look down and see a pool of blood covering the soles of his feet barely going over his toes. Markus would walk around the statues confused where he is as he sees a reflective world across from him with cloaked statues. As he walks over to the mirror to see the cloaked statues a figure appears before him. Markus is surprised and panics and he stumbles back and falls on his butt. He looks up at the figure and realizes it is himself, but in his trench coat and mask. Markus gets up and looks into the red fiery eyes that glow with power and death before the figure speaks. "You are weak. You have let these criminals continue their terror, you let the corrupted system survive." Markus raises an eyebrow. "I am trying to uncorrupt the system. I am fighting for the people who cower in fear of these men. No one was safe before me, before we gave them hope." "Did DJ see it that way? We have to end this. Take the power from the corrupted and use them to make something new. Something better." "Freedom and Justice is the best system out there. They just need to be clean." Kronos walks out of the mirror towards Markus then looks at the statues. "You fight for order. But we create chaos. You defend people's freedom, but we enslave the wrongdoers. Let me take control and we don't need to worry about the future of humanity." Markus looks to the statues to his sides as thinks about his actions. The Statues start to crack. "N-No. I will not. I am in control. I will not let monsters roam free. I will fix the system. There can be peace and justice. There can be freedom, even if I am the sole protector of it." Kronos walks back to the mirror. "I see. When you lose your way. When you can no longer help the people your way. You know where to find me." Kronos says this with a grin under his mask, returning to the other side of the mirror. Markus wakes up in a sweet as he looks around his room. The conversation with "himself" would remain in his mind for some time as he looks at himself in the mirror. "I am doing this so my friends, my family, don't suffer the same fate as Sasha." Markus puts the mask on as his blue eyes and line glows.

CHAPTER

11

FRIENDS TO RIVALS

A few days after the bank robbery, the City had remained with a terrifying silence. No crime, no firefights, no signs of any gang. It was a silent week. For some, a time to reflect.

DJ would be walking the streets, much more cautiously, but in a serious tone he had never held. He walks into a hospital that was along his route and walks to the desk asking the clerk if he can see his friend. The Clerk would allow him with a smile. DJ would go up three floors and arrive at room 3097. Before walking in, two adults would walk out. The woman had dirty blonde hair with lightly tan skin and the man had brown hair with hazel eyes. They see DJ and look at him with a sad smile. The father would speak up. "Hello Dany. Good to see some of her friends still see her." DJ looks at them a bit upset himself. "How is she doing? Still in a coma?" The mother looked down before speaking. "Yes. We don't understand why. Maybe the shock of pain was too much?" "That is what the doctor believes." The father says before holding his wife close. DJ would retreat to his serious face before any tears start to flow. "She will snap out of it. I know she will. She is strong, one of the strongest I know." The mother smiles a bit and walks away as the father shakes DJ's hand. "Thank you Dany. She was lucky to have you and... Markus when he lived." Leaves soon after saying that with some grief. DJ would walk into the room, looking at the girl in the bed. It was Sasha, alive, but in a coma. DJ sits by her bed and sighs with sadness. "Hey Sasha. How are you holding up? Good I hope. Please hang in there." DJ would continue talking to her for a while and then goes into the bank robbery scene, he speaks of Markus's rescue, describing him as some vigilante of fear. He then stands and walks to the window. "Reminds me of when you and Markus came into my life. Remember?"

Years ago during their middle school days DJ lived in a bad neighborhood with a few gangs residing in the area. DJ had been walking down with his head down and scared. Meanwhile Sasha would be skipping down the street to see some friends. Markus, a bit away, had slipped away from his family with a BB gun playing cop. As DJ walks down the street he turns into a group of bigger boys. He doesn't see them and bumps into them, falling to the ground sniffing as he scrapes his arm. The boys turn to him. "Watch it twerp. You're gonna dirty my clothes." "Look man, the kid is filthy he must have dirtied your clothes." The other boy would wipe his hoodie. The kids were all dark skin and in high school by the looks of them. While Markus was running around the neighborhood shooting at random bottles and cans he would hear the bullies. Sasha would hear them too as she skips down the street with her backpack. Markus and Sasha slow down and get upset. Markus becomes angry as he rushes over. Sasha would become worried as she too rushed over to see what was going on. The bullies pick DJ up and surround him. "You are gonna pay for that twerp. Perhaps with blood." Markus rounds the corner and sees the bullies about to punch him. He raises his BB pistol up and shoots into the bullies legs causing him to flinch and drop DJ onto his feet. "Freeze punk! You are being mean." The bullies laugh as they move over. Sasha sees them and runs over to DJ checking his arm. Markus would shoot them with his BB gun and aims for the main one's privates. The bullies would flinch in pain as they were shot at. The main bully would be hit in the privates and hold them before limping away. "This kid is a dangerous dawg!" "We outta here. He ain't worth it." They all run out of his line of sight. Markus smirks and then goes over to the others. "Hey kid, you ok?" Sasha looks at his arm. "He is hurt, we can take him to my friend's mother, she can help." They held the DJ, who was tearing up. They would bring him to the family that ended up helping him. Returning to DJ looking out the window, he was smiling. "Who knew we would be in the same middle school? That was a great way to meet my best friends. Now one is dead and the other in a coma." He walks back to Sasha, sitting in the chair. "I can't lose another friend. Keep fighting Sasha. I know Markus would want that." DJ spends an hour talking about all their adventures and how they became the closest of friends. Even speaking of the day Markus and Sasha became lovers. "When Markus told me, it was pretty funny at first. Then I could see it was a good match. Though I must admit I wish I had something like that." He would go on and on about many things until a doctor walked in. "Doctor, is there any idea if she will come out?" "Hm? Don't worry mr. Davis. Her mind just needs to process what is happening and heal. She will be out of it soon." DJ sighs and stands up. "I will see you again Sasha. Wake soon." DJ would leave as the Doctor would check on her before having nurses tend to her. DJ walks out of the hospital. Before leaving the area he looks up at the building with hope. Meanwhile hope shines brightest at the hospital where the farm where Markus and his Legion is based is shrouded in darkness. Markus would be sitting in a chair thinking. "I must find Cerberus. I will kill him, I will get vengeance for Sasha, but first I will learn why he dared to cross my path that dark day." His eyes were red before he took a breath and closed his eyes. Opening them once more to show his blue eyes. "Time to move." He gets up and puts his mask on. Walking out of the master room, with Buck and his Knights ready and waiting for him.

CHAPTER

12

POISONOUS TREAT

Cerberus would stand at a table looking at all of his operations, the areas he controls. The areas he barely holds. His operations have slowed so much that their contractors and illegal businessmen have halted any payment and even denied Cerberus any jobs. His credibility had dropped so low he could barely hold his gang together. A drifting gap between the loyal members and those who want to strike out on their own. Cerberus would think of any possible way to rid themselves of the Legion and the annoyance they were so grand at making. "How do they keep getting more members? How do they grow and even know all our bases? How!?" He would be puzzled.

While Cerberus spent most of his time alone. His loyal officers would be looking into every spot. Attempting to shine their lights on the Legion. Though the Legion of Darkness lived up to their name. After some time the HellHounds Officers would finally get something. A few of their men come into their meeting as they were discussing how to find the Legion and deal them the same distress they were in. "Hey, sorry to barge in but we got a few areas we were watching. We finally got some. A few Legion boys walked into some places." Intrigued, the officer let them come to the table with a map of everything. They point to four locations. A docking area, two warehouses, and a condemned church building. "awesome!" One of the officers shouts. "This will show those Legion scumbags that we ain't going out without some blood." While all but one officer cheered in agreement, the lone officer would think as the others left to get their men ready. "Four spots in one day? I doubt they got that sloppy." One of his men walks up. "Bossman, we have their locations, we could deal them some major pain." "Even so it seems… too easy. Something is wrong, but I can't see how." The other Officers would take their men as they leave for the zones. "Let's give them some blood!" Of all six officers only one remained behind. He would call Cerberus and explain the situation. The closest spot would be a warehouse off a few blocks from where they were meeting. "Shitheads have been under our noses this whole time." One of the HellHounds said as they all moved in. They see no guards, no cameras, and nothing of value. Leaving many confused as they enter the warehouse. Markus was on the upper platform watching them enter. He then claps, slowly. His claps caused them all to jump and look up at him. "Well well, you found me. I didn't expect you all to be this foolish. Must have you all on the edge." Instead of replying they fill him with holes as they fire every round they have into him. Flinching to every shot Markus is pushed to the wall and slides down it as if he had died. The HellHounds grin and congratulate themselves before hearing small metal objects hitting the ground. Markus gets up as the bullets are forced out of his body. He looks at his coat and clothes. "You put holes in my clothes. Seems everyone here is too trigger happy. Isn't that right Reyes." Reyes would walk over and sit on some small crates with her wolf, Waffles. "Indeed. I say they deserve some righteous punishment, Lord Kronos." She laughs as she pets Waffles. Her laughter is joined with the chilling and terrifying laughter of the Gremlins. The HellHounds split between paralyzed with fear or jumping around terrified. Markus crosses his arms looking down at them. One of them tries to call the other crews. As he is making the call his phone drains fast before powering off.

Markus smirks under his mask. "I wouldn't bother. Your friends are in their own traps made by my most skilled Knights." The HellHounds attempt to open the doors and bash their way out, with no luck. The Gremlins would rush in as the lights dimmed into complete darkness. Only the eyes of the gremlins would be seen. A red gremlin would look into the eyes of the officer and see his nightmare. His nightmare happened to be a large snake that would eat him. One would appear behind him. Hearing it's his he turns and drops to the ground yelling. One of his men came over trying to pick him up "cap'n?" The officer would not hear him as he hears only a hiss coming towards him he pulls his gun and fires at the snake, who happens to be his own man. Soon Gremlins would drag away some, killing, ripping, and eating the dead men. Others would experience their nightmares and would kill one another. While death and carnage consume the lives of the HellHounds there, the other locations the HellHounds targeted would meet similar fates. The second warehouse the HellHounds visit have a few guards, their mark of enslavement seen by the HellHounds as they move in and shoot at them. The slaves, putting up a fight, as they draw their pistols and fire back. The exchange of gunfire would bring the attention of police quicker than expected. The slaves retreat into the warehouse after some losses. The remaining HellHounds move in with their officer leading the charge. They would walk into a line of Knights looking down the sights of semi automatic rifles. Within moments the officer and most of his boys were laying on the floor, or on each other, dead. The few left would be surprised by the Police, rolling in sirens blaring. They hop out and draw their guns yelling "FREEZE!"

Moving up to the HellHounds who drop their guns as they lose the will to fight. As they are arrested they tell them of the massacre in the warehouse. A few police slowly investigate and only see a warehouse of dead bodies. Putting a heavy weight on their minds and hearts. "Damn… this gang war is more like… just war." While they search the warehouse the Knights are sneaking out through a secret opening with Buck smirking. "Lord Kronos sends his thanks, officers." He says to himself. He would follow his men out and hide the opening before police entered slowly searching the warehouse. Meanwhile the same would be happening in an abandoned apartment complex. This team is led by Greg McAllister. The last place the HellHounds rushed to was empty. Only a few Legion Slaves, there to greet them with a gun fight. Though a few HellHounds died, the slaves were quickly killed as well. Back at the Farm Markus, Buck, and Greg waited for Jones. "He is late…" Markus said as a Legion slave rushes in and falls to his knee in front of Markus. "Master the third location was understaffed. The few slaves there were killed." "And where is Jones? Who I put in command of the ambush force I left." Markus says curious, yet a bit angered. "He was spotted at the memorial Hermman hospital." Markus would sigh before walking off. "Follow me Buck and Greg."

The three make their way to the hospital and enter in street clothes. Buck goes to the receptionist. "Excuse me, has a Jones Hall been here? We set up a meet up and he didn't come, one of his friends said he came here." "Hm let me check." The woman behind the counter said. "Here, Rebecca Halls. He should be in there." The guys look at each other. Markus would give some Phantoms the chance to search for them and return within a few seconds. "I see. Thank you ma'am, can we see them?" Markus asks, pushing his shades up close to his face. "I am afraid she is only here to see family. You will have to wait." "No worries, we can see him later." Markus says as he walks out with the two waving goodbye to the receptionist. They would walk around to the back and climb up a level with the help of the gremlins acting like a ladder. "They are scary and useful. "Greg says climbing them as they enter the room where Jones sits with a woman. Markus walks over. "Jones. What are you doing here?" Buck asks, a bit worried. Jones turns to them and gets up to bow to Markus. "I am sorry my lord I was set to attack the HellHound bastards… but I received word from the doctors that my wife is getting worse." Greg would think for a moment. "What does she have?" "No idea. She went to a party held by the HellHounds… she didn't know. Just wanted to go with her friends… She took some drugs. The Drug seems to have a quick addiction, she took a bit too much cause her friends were being horrible influences. Now." He holds her cheek. "The drugs seem to be too much and the doctors fear she will start losing organs. All shutting down one by one. She only asks for a few days." While Buck and Greg try to cheer up Jones and talk in the background, Shadow speaks to Markus alone. "Master, Jones is a loyal servant and his anger would be power. Though if you wish, take some of your gremlin's life force and heal her." "And what of my gremlins?" Markus whispers as he looks to his shoulder with no one there. "We can make more." Markus nods and holds his loyal hand up to her as white light glows from his hand gaining the attention of the others. At the cost of four gremlins Rebecca would slowly recover and heal. Markus stops as he breathes heavily and stumbles. Greg and Buck hold him as Jones goes to Rebecca. She starts to wake and smiles at Jones. "Jones. I missed you." Jones starts to tear up and smiles. "I missed you too, I am happy you are better." They hug and embrace each other for a bit allowing Markus to stand tall again. Jones breaks the hug. "While you were... dying. I met some people who were helping people like us from drugs and criminals. Meet Lord Kronos, Buck, and Greg. Thank you my lord. For this gift." Rebecca, confused at first, smiles at Markus. "If you healed me, I think we owe you much. If you are a Lord, allow us to serve you." Markus smiles. "No need. Jones has helped our cause enough, he deserves love. And I am not in the market for letting innocents die thanks to the inhuman actions of drug lords." Rebecca thinks for a moment. "If I may my lord, thanks to you our girls and son still have a mother. Our family owes you and would love to help." Jones steps in. "Might as well give in my Lord. She is persistent." Markus laughs. "Very well, I was thinking of spreading our good will to those on the verge of drugs or addicted to drugs... and who better than a survivor." She nods as she pulls Jones in for a kiss. Markus and the others would leave through the window they came through and let them go. Later on they learn that Rebecca is still weak, but recovering. The doctors would be surprised as the news hears of her miracle recovery.

A week later Rebecca has a few news teams asking her and her doctors what happened. She would step up and speak. "I was visited by a man of miracles. He heard the pleas of my husband and saved me, but even a man of miracles has limits. I wish to tell you all out there, that these drug dealers are criminals... no, terrorists known as the HellHounds pose with these drugs. To those who are addicted seek help before you end up in the dying state I was in." These words would bring attention to the HellHounds and their drugs.

CHAPTER

13

A STEP UP

Weeks after the Miracle of Kronos, people's views and public opinion of the Legion of Darkness rises. Nearly half the city is supportive of these "vigilantes", as the people call them. Most crime was conducted by the HellHounds within the city. Though now the wave of crime the city endured for years has dropped to near nothing.

Meanwhile Cerberus stands in his office looking into the city. "These Legion boys were underestimated. A poor choice of ours. This city was mine. It will be again." He goes to his table and leans against it. He picks up his phone and calls someone. "Hello. I am calling in a favor. If you wish to continue your goal, and the money we supply, you will get us help. I will get my boys to drop off the grid for a bit. Get the Legion out of our city." He takes a moment on the phone listening to whoever he called. "Sounds good to me. I know I can handle them afterwards." He hangs up and looks out the window. Within weeks HellHounds are gone from the streets and the Legion members would be confused.

Days after a stop in HellHound activity the club that Reyes owns is visited by a group of men in suits, as well as a woman with brown hair in a ponytail and hazel eyes. She was in a suit as she walked towards the club with four men in tow. The bouncer stops them. "You ain't invited." The woman speaks up. "This is a club right? People can walk in." "Not when they are in suits." "Agent Morse, FBI we would like to talk to your club owner. Miss Tonki?" The bouncer glares at her and scoffs at the idea of letting her in but lets her through. "Upstairs." He says, displeased. They Walk into the club as people party without a worry. Morse would watch the party for a moment before walking upstairs. Another bouncer stops them. Before he could say anything the door behind him opens as Reyes looks down at the agents, a bit surprised. "Oh Hello there. Are you clients?" Morse would show her badge quickly, though Reye's eyes notice a black stripe on the badge. "FBI. We are here to investigate the HellHounds and Legion of Darkness. Mind if we talk about the Club attack the HellHounds made?" Reyes would sketch every detail of the agents into her eyes as she stands there listening. "I had already talked to the Police about that-" "Their report has been read, however we need to investigate ourselves." Morse interrupts as she gets closer to Reye's desk and leans on it. "I want to know what REALLY happened." Reyes would show her distaste for the agent. "Hands off my desk. I gave my report. Leave. Now." She sternly says, not backing down from Morse. Morse would get off the desks taking her leave slowly. "Whatever you are hiding, we will find it." Reyes would stare at Morse as she and her agents leave. She had been threatened in her own club and was forced to let them walk away. Fuming with anger she would call Markus. "Kronos. The FBI are investigating. Be careful."

A few days pass. Kronos had been hunting the HellHounds to extinction, but their sudden disappearance worried him. Almost as much as the FBI showing up. His men would search the city for their adversaries. Eventually a group of Legion find some HellHounds. In the middle of a street, HellHounds would stumble into five Legion members. At the sight of each other they draw their guns and start firing away, causing a panic in the area as people scream. The gang fight would be pulled into an alleyway as the Legion members try to get the fight out of the streets and away from the people. The HellHounds lose some men before running away. Before the Legion could pursue, FBI and Police cars blockaded the alleyway. The Legion boys try to bust through a locked backdoor but only run into Agent Morse and a lot of armed men. "FREEZE! On the ground!" The five men would leap at the officers. More officers show up and pin the five men, taking them to the police station. As the Officers arrest the members of the Legion of Darkness. Purple mist hovered in the corner of the room. The mist solidifies into a phantom gremlin, standing on a shelf in the dim lightened corner. Through the eyes of the gremlin he would see the chain markings on four of their heads and a sword marking on the last member. Snarling, the Gremlin would turn back to mist and return to Markus.

Hours later. Thornvel and Gordon would be watching the FBI interrogating the Legion members. The current one being a slave. "Where is your leader? Tell us and you can get a pardon." The agent says calmly. The slave would stare off into space ignoring the agent. "Look. You were caught by multiple eyewitnesses that saw you shooting. We can at least lower your charges." The agent says a bit aggravated. The slave remains silent. Not a drop of sweat. Thronvel would shake her head. "We have been at this for hours. They won't talk." Gordon nods agreement. "Must be some loyalty to their leader. Wonder why." They both sigh and watch as they switch the slave out for the loyalist. They spend hours trying to get any information. Until Morse walked into the interrogation room. She slams a small folder on the table. "I'm sick of this loyalty B.S. your boss ain't coming for you. So you can either be locked up for life doing hard times, or tell me what I want and get an early sentence." The man just holds his hands together and sits quietly. A smirk on his face forms to mock her. Morse would sit calmly across from him. "I am Amanda Morse. Captain in the FBI. I have plenty of pull, so tell me and-" the man pulls his hand up to stop her before cupping them together once more. "Nothing you say or do will make me betray the trust of my 'boss'. The others will be less willing. So drop it." Morse is displeased as she stands up. She walks over to the camera and turns it off. "I also have plenty of pull to do this." She would bring in some of her agents and lock the door. The loyalist shakes his head. The agents would beat on the Loyalist and attempt to break him.

Meanwhile at the Farm Markus would be thinking of the FBI capturing one of the loyalists. Buck and Jones were in the same room waiting, along with Shadow. "So the FBI caught our men in a gunfight with the HellHounds. Then the FBI captured ONLY them and not the HellHounds? What the hell is going on?" Jones steps forward and speaks. "My Lord, shouldn't we rescue our loyal knight? If we abandon him the others might be concerned." "No worries Jones. I want you and Buck to investigate. Take some knights and get our man out. If you can take the slaves too. The more numbers we have the better. Plus it would be weird if only one of our men was broken out." They nod and walk out of the room and begin planning. Markus stands in the room with Shadow, sitting in a nearby chair.

"Shadow, find out everything about this FBI agent that has threatened my loyal knights. And threatened Miss Tonka." His eyes turn red once more as he stares outside the window in the room. "No one! No one threatens my people!" Shadow would smile as he disappeared into the shadows.

While Buck and his forces plan a breakout of their men, loyals and slaves alike, Amanda Morse had spent the day getting information that would never come. She and her agents roughed up all the Legion members. She sat in the Police captain's office with Thornvel and Gordon. "Their loyalty is surprisingly strong. Even a common crook is not this loyal." The captain looks to Thronvel. "My officers here believe there is more to this. And I believe them. As many other officers have voiced their concerns about the Legion." Amanda laughs. "Captain. you can't be serious? The Legion is just another gang. One, your officers failed to control and decided to make up excuses." Gordon steps forward, angered. "There is no excuse. Often in Legion turf our officers get a cold chill like someone… or something is watching us. Besides that, what about the reports of mass missing persons?" Amanda bites back. "Keep your officers in line, or perhaps they need some discipline." The captain looks angered as well. The tension between the police captain and FBI captain would fill the station. "My Officers kept the peace before and are more than enough. I have no idea why the Governor called in you. I don't even know what branch of the FBI you are." "That is classified" Amanda injected into the conversation. The Police Captain Seemed to give up and stood up. "Fine, but my officers will do what they believe is right." He would par Gordon's shoulder before moving to open the door. "Now I have reports to file and things to do. Please leave." Amanda, still confident and superior, walks out of the office. The captain slams the door behind her and sits in his chair sighing annoyed. Gordon would move to the front of the desk. "Sorry captain. I should have held my tongue." "That woman is too prideful. She believes her agents are big shots. Even her own agents think the same. Working together will be hard." Thornvel would move over. "Sir, let us investigate the Legion." The captain thinks for a moment, worried for his officers. His thoughts weigh on the Legion and FBI being a danger. After a long thought of the situation he would speak up. "No, the risk is too great. Captain Morse seems a bit ruthless and may put you two in danger if she knew what you were doing. As for the Legion, let them deal with the FBI. We might not like the idea. But it is the best course." Thornvel would disagree but forced herself to comply. "Yes... sir." Gordon notices this and salutes the captain, with Thornvel doing the same after. They leave the office and talk in private. "Thornvel, you are not thinking-" "yes I am. We know this city and we can do better than the FBI. Let's get the info the FBI needs and then we can impress the captain. Show them Police are just as good as them." Gordon thinks for a moment and sighs. His heart knew she would go anyway. "Alright, but we do this smart and slow. We can't let the captain or anyone else know." Thornvel nods in agreement. Though Gordon would begin to fear what is to come.

CHAPTER

14

TRUTH AND DARE

The FBI and Police had been working towards information on the Legion. While the Legion would be planning a Jailbreak led by Buck. Often scooping out the Police station. The FBI and Legion would be looking to make the next move. Taking time to plan or gain info, while Thornvel and Gordon do their own investigation. The shift between fighting a gang to fighting the government changed the strategy of battle within the Legion.

Gordon and Thornvel would be driving in their car, planning. "Alright so where should we start?" Asks Gordon driving the car. "Well, we should start with the club. It is a major part of this gang's rise." Gordon nods and makes his way to the club. "Think Miss Tonka will help anymore?" Thornvel would think for a moment before shaking her head. "No, I don't think so. She gave what she could. I think." "Couldn't hurt to ask." They arrive at the club as FBI agents leave. One of the agents memorizes their faces as he stares at them passing by the club. Thornvel would stare back for a moment. "We should take the back entrance that Miss Tonka showed before." Gordon would agree as they go to the back entry way. As they arrive Reyes would be leaving and getting into a car with her personal guards. The guards would happen to have Legion attire. "Wait, thought Miss Tonka wasn't with them?" Gordon would be shocked yet confused. "Maybe she is a hostage. But we should tail them." Thornvel would write down the details and license plate. As Reyes leaves in the black SUV. Thornvel and Gordon would follow them. Within the city there would be plenty of cars to keep eyes off the two officers. Once they would start to leave the city Gordon and Thornvel were confused as they continued to follow. Though as soon as they neared the farmlands the SUV took twists and turns to lose the two. "Damn it. Pull off and head back to the city. Act normal." Gordon would continue on the main path as the SUV would return now behind them. Gordon then takes a turn and then makes his way to the city. "Why are they all the way out here? It is just farms." Thornvel would be in deep thought. She would look in her wide mirror and see the SUV continue on the road. "Maybe family? Or maybe the Legion took up a base here. We should look into any abandoned or recent purchases in the last year." Gordon would nod as Thornvel looks into any info through their car's personal computer.

As soon as Thornvel and Gordon get back to base they would be greeted by a fellow officer with an upset look. "The captain wants you two in his office." They would look at each other worried. As they walk to the captain's office they would see FBI agents gearing up with automatic rifles and shotguns. Entering the Captain's office, they see Amanda and their captain talking. Their captain would leave the room in a disappointed huff. Amanda would lean against the captain's desk. "Sit officers. we need to have a little chat." They sit begrudgingly. Amanda walks around them as she begins to spout her disappointment. "You two are reckless. Taking a Police vehicle to a Legion controlled area. My agents that were watching the club and Miss Tonka reported you two and how after looking into the club for our target she was gone. So since you ruined our chance, I would hope you two have some information. You share that and I will share something for you two. Plus you two will keep your jobs." They remain quiet until Gordon speaks up. "It was my idea." Thornvel would be surprised. "Gordon, you know that is not true." He holds his hand up to shush Thornvel. "It was my idea. We tailed Miss Tonka through a back way into her club. An alleyway big enough for some cars. A little parking area big enough for a couple cars. We followed them out of the city towards the farmland northeast of here." Thornvel would be upset with Gordon. Amanda would smile. "Well done. You two would be better agents than police, but with that. I have information on a prison break targeting the Legion members in this station. Not sure where they are stationed but if our timing is right the Police AND the FBI can take down this gang. Cooperate and you will get all the glory." Though Thornvel did not like Amanda she would sigh, looking at Gordon before turning her stare at Amanda. "Fine, but our captain deserves that glory." "Fine by me. I will take Reyes Tonka, I can send some agents to find their base in the farmlands. You two and some fellow police can capture these prison breakers." They nod in agreement. Amanda would have the captain and many others in on the plan. The station would gear up in swat armor and weapons. Within the day they would find the locations they needed. Mobilizing to capture or kill the Legion of Darkness.

Buck would be with his men finishing their own plans. "The school bus can join up with the real school buses after we arrive at the extraction point." There would be nearly two dozen men in the room. "After we get our man and the punished we can solidify Lord Kronos as a protector. Remember we are not to kill the officers. They are just doing their job. But we will free our brother." They all agree. Before they would move from their spots, a door opened slightly, creaking and taking the attention of the Knights. A flashbang is tossed into the room. Buck and the others dive for cover or drop to the ground as the flash goes off blinding and deafening them. Swat and police move into the room en masse. They would yell and pin many of them down. By the time the Knights recovered, they were already in cuffs. "What the fuck?" "You have a right to remain silent, I suggest you use it." They are read their rights before the officers start to corral them into police cars and swat trucks. The local people are shocked. Seeing the Legion members arrested would cause some cheering and some booing. The people seem to be divided in opinion of the Legion, this would be burnt into the officers minds. Just as Buck and his men are arrested. The FBI used the back way into the club to arrest Reyes and her men. Some of which were Legion knights and slaves. They breach into Reyes's office as she looks at them with disgust. "You dare break into my club!? Agent Morse will suffer greatly for this." Amanda would walk into the room. "I highly doubt that Miss Tonka. Hope you like your future cell cause you will be there for a long time. Not the king anymore huh?" Reyes would laugh a bit to mock Morse. "I am the Queen. The King is a different story. And you will never beat him." Morse would be annoyed and had her men arrest her. "He will join you soon then." Meanwhile at the Farm Markus would be looking at a map. "The HellHounds are gone. Disappeared. That doesn't make sense." Markus receives a call from a police officer "My Lord, Police and FBI have mobilized. I tried to get away to call. They are heading to the farm!" Markus looks surprised, rushing out of his room speaking to his men.

"Get the Slaves armed and defenses up." Shadow prepares the bunker. Hold the line for a few minutes before retreating into the Bunker. Having choke points is better." The knight nods and goes outside. The slaves take automatic and semi automatic guns getting behind cover and setting up. The Helicopters arrive first, with black armored FBI SWAT descending from them. As they descend the Legion opens fire on them shooting them off the helicopters. The helicopters would pull away. "They are armed, lethal force authorized." A pilot says before taking a bullet to the head. The helicopter spins, sending some of its passengers flying as it crashes into the crop field. The SUVs arrive as agents unload and rush up to the walls of the Legion compound. Legion slaves man the walls and fire down at the agents. Killing a few of them before the agents throw flashbangs and shoot back. A few slaves would be killed. Markus would watch this. He would then order them to pull back to the bunker as he steps out with his pistols. Agents would bring up a handheld ram and bust down the gate as they moved into the courtyard shooting at the Legion. Markus would fire at them with his pistols, taking out a few as his men retreated into the farmhouse and down to the bunker they constructed. After his men got inside Markus would pull back taking shots to his chest and limbs. Before walking down to the bunker. The agents would be confused. "I swear we shot that masked man more than enough." "Maybe he has kevlar?" They debate it as they move into the house and then see the hole in the ground. They would move down it as some stayed to search the other rooms. They enter a dark tunnel. Turning their lights on they see a vault-like door in front of them. They would begin to get it open as their flashlights start losing power. Slowly dying. "What is wrong with these things?" Gremlin laughter would be heard. Sending chills down all of their spines. Some shiver in fear. "What the fuck? They… they must be using speakers to… to freak us out." They hear screams from upstairs. Their lights went out as darkness shrouded them. Panic sets in as they see the yellow and red eyes of their killers. They fire randomly trying to kill the yellow and red eyes though often kill their own. The few lucky ones run out of the tunnel and into the house only to be met by a large 8 foot tall green hairy beast. The beast gremlin bashes the agents to the walls as the others pin them and tie them up. As the vault opens Legion men step into the tunnel with their own flashlights seeing the carnage that befell the agents. Some were filled with bullets while others were cut and ripped into pieces. They would return to the open area now only holding the few captured Agents that were sent to raid them. Markus would walk towards the agents as Shadow appeared on his shoulder. The Agents are consumed by fear and horror as they gaze on Shadow. "Master these Agents have taken Lady Reyes and your Knight Commander has not reported for his rescue." "I see. Let's see what these men have done." Markus raises both hands but only his hand with the chain glows to each of them. He would brand them all and would tell Markus what they have done. "So you all are guilty of crimes against the people? Torturing, assassinating, blackmail, bribes!? I was not aware that the government had such corruption. Reyes mentioned Captain Morse? Tell me about her!" An agent bows. "Agent Amanda Morse is captain of our unit. She is currently taking Reyes Tonka to the Police station along with every Legion Member within the prison break group and in Lady Reyes's company." Markus would slowly anger. "Why are you here?" "To destroy the Legion under the Governor's request. More details are with Morse." Markus would burn with rage as his eyes turned red. "Then I suppose I should visit your captain. Men stay and guard the base. Contact all Legion members in the city to be vigilant and prepare for a city in chaos. The police and These agents are no longer worthy of protecting the people. We will be justice!" His men cheer their lord on, even his new slaves. Markus would take an Agent SUV and drive towards the city.

The Police station would be filled with Legion prisoners and celebrating officers. Amanda would be interrogating Reyes with Gordon, Thornvel and their captain watching. "We took a lot of Legion members. But there are still more. I am sure the farm is already done and on their way here. So want to shorten your sentence? Spill the other locations." Reyes would scoff. "First, where's Waffles?" "In a cage with the Legion prisoners. You won't see him for a long time." Amanda opens a file and looks at a record of Reyes. As they interrogate Reyes and some others Markus arrives at the Police station and stands right outside the doors. "Shadow. Let us give them a chance to surrender. If they don't comply, kill them. We will burn this station to the ground!" A horde of Gremlins exit the shadows within the station. Preparing to kill and burn. Power would be flickering as lights and computers flicker. Reyes smiles. "I think I will be seeing my Waffles soon. The King is here." The intercoms would turn on as Markus speaks through them. "I am Lord Kronos, leader of the Legion of Darkness. You have taken my loyal Knights and my advisor. I will give you ten minutes to bring them out to me. Failure to comply will be unwise." The police station is filled with Legion cheers and rattling the bars they would begin a chant. "Kronos! Kronos! Kronos!" The police would be surprised. Arming up as a few go out to arrest Kronos. "Down on the ground! Now!" Markus would glare at them sending a stone cold chill freezing them. Their breaths stalled before they began to panic. Every instinct is telling them to run. "You dare! I gave you plenty of time. But you deny me. You DEFY ME!" He draws his guns and shoots at two of the five officers. The last three shoot at Markus filling him with holes. But Markus stands still as he guns them down. The camera witnessing this would send the station into a panic. "He... he should be dead! What happened?" Suddenly power shuts off as the only light left would be emergency power and light from the sun as the station is overrun with Gremlins eating, cutting, and beating the Officers and Agents. The officers would kill a few gremlins, but would be quickly overrun. Markus walks into the Police station and shoots a few other officers who attempt to stop him. Screams and gunfire filled the station as death claimed so many. The Legion knights and slaves would be released by Shadow. As they pick up guns and start to kill or capture officers and agents. Amanda would walk out with some of her agents toward the captain's office. "Get this station under control he must had beaten our agents and had his men attack the station." She would begin to hear reports of the gremlins. Though she would not believe it. "They are only men! They are not demons or-" she would hear the men on the radios getting overwhelmed as Laughter filled the Radio channel. Thornvel and Gordon would move with their captain towards the front entrance. They would see a few gremlin shockers tazing some of their officers into an unconscious state before they turned their gaze at the group. Thornvel and Gordon fire at them, killing one of them before the others run and hide. "What are they!?" Thornvel yells, scared to death. "Whatever they are, they are killable." Gordon is a little calmer than Thornvel. They would escort the captain and they would keep an eye out for more. A few phantoms would start fires or make explosions within the station, gaining the attention of outside viewers. Chaos consumes the station as even officers, loyal or enslaved, run on their fellow officers. Gordon, Thornvel, and their captain see a few officers cuffing their fellow officers. Two Legion officers would sneak up on the group. "sorry cap'n, but you are under arrest." Thornvel is shocked and turns sharply. "What is the meaning of this!?" "Thornvel, Gordon. You two are good officers and you should join the Legion. Lord Kronos is the future." Gordon would become curious. "How is he the future? He is just a man." The Legion officers speak with conviction and pride. "He is more than a man. He is hope, he is the spark to end crime. Even our crooked cops will be punished." Thornvel yells at him angered. "How can you say that when you are killing good officers!?" They turn to her. "We are killing those who stand in our way. We will keep as many as possible." A few gremlins would be dragging in unconscious police and turn to their allies. "Capture for da master!" As the two officers turn Gordon makes a move to take them down. Punching the closest one. "Get the captain out! Go!" Thronvel would kick the other man. "I won't leave you Gordon!" The captain shoots at the gremlins, though they escape his shots. Gordon would shoot the Legion officer he was fighting. "Captain, take Leia and go!" The captain looks to Gordon and then around the room. Seeing the other Legion members, officers, and gremlins moving to intercept them. He would realize that staying meant certain death. He looks to Gordon and nods before taking Thronvel's arm and pulling her. "Thronvel we need to go!" She struggles, yet pulls back with the captain as she watches Gordon be jumped by Gremlins, stabbing into him with knives. "Lucas!" She yells in anger and sadness. As she leaves out the front doors with the captain and runs into the city. The yelling of her partner would reach her and haunt her, along with the laughter of the monsters that took him. Only a few minutes later did Markus reach the captain's room walking in as if he owned the place. He would see three agents pointing their MP5s at his chest. Amanda Morse sat in the captain's chair filled with anger, yet surprised. "For a gangbanger you have some balls. No way a dumbass will get away with this. The FBI will hunt you down." Markus's red eyes flare up as if enraged. He then snaps his fingers as Shadow comes out and drags one of the agents into his shadow. Markus would use the surprise to kick the other in the head, knocking them to the ground as he back kicks the other into the wall and punches the agent until he couldn't take anymore. The two agents lay on the ground in pain. "I am no gangbanger. I am Lord Kronos, your soon to be master." "You think some show of force will make you my leader!?" She laughs before becoming enraged again, slamming her fist to the table. "Shut the fuck up and listen to this dipshit. You have nowhere to hide. This city will see your Legion as monsters, hell they will never let you go free. No one will cover for you." Shadow returns from the shadows as he walks on the desk. Amanda keeps her cool. "Master, this one is pure evil! She has seen the gates of the underworld and has sent many people. Innocent or guilty to its realm. She can be useful." Markus turns to Amanda as he looks to the windows and nods. A few moments later two of his men walk in and pull Amanda out of her chair and put her on her knees. Markus holds his enslavement hand to her head, though the chain would become a broken dagger design. He presses it against her head as she screams in pain. "You will become my infiltrator and you will fight for MY name!" Markus would pull his hand off her head. She would stand and bow. "What do you wish of me, master?" Markus smirks under his mask as he places his hands behind him. He sits in the captain chair. "Men clear the police station. Make it seem we are aiding the police. Inform the others outside to help the people." The knights nod and leave. Markus turns his gaze onto Amanda. He leans forward and cups his hands together. "What branch of the FBI are you?" Amanda, now a thrall, turns to her master and gladly explains. "I am not part of the FBI, we use the FBI when making open claims and working with police or media. We are known as the Hunter Initiative. We hunt down those who gain too much power within our country. We condone blackmail, illegal actions, assassinations, and much more. We are the dark side of the government that controls this country. If an op goes wrong or we are discovered we put someone else in sight of the police to be arrested. A scapegoat. Sometimes if our organization is as openly, acting as the FBI and messes up we terminate a fake Director, usually an old criminal where we erase their records."

All this information surprised Markus as he listened deeply. "Why was this 'Hunter Initiative' sent after us? We were just a 'gang'." Amanda would pull out her phone. "We are known by few. The Governor of Texas, Alexander Leathers, contacted us and put a hit on the Legion. We learned that it wasn't because of your increase in power, but as a favor to one of his supporters I was supposed to bring down your Legion and find the supporter to find dirt on him." Markus's blue eyes return after much thought. "You have two orders then. First, hunt down the police and Hunters that fled the station or weren't here. You are to act as a survivor. Your second order find corruption among their ranks or even with the governor. We can use this to our advantage." She bows. "Yes my Lord." She says before walking away. Markus would stand from the chair and walk out of the office. Heading to the top where some of his loyal Officers held a haul of Police and Hunter Agents. Markus would brand all the Hunter Agents, yet only half of the captured police officers. The last few would be in awe of his power. Only a couple would offer allegiance, and meant it. The last few were sent to the prison cells as they cleaned up and fixed the station. Buck, Reyes, and her pet Waffles walk over to Markus. Reyes playing with her bloodied wolf. Markus turns to them. "Glad to see you are all safe. Did we lose anyone?" "Some loyal officers and Knights, but only five." Buck says with grief for his fallen brothers. Markus places a hand on his shoulder. "Their sacrifice will not be in vain." He then turns to Reyes and her wolf. "Glad to see you are ok." Reyes stands up and hugs Markus. "Thank you for the rescue, that woman Agent Morse was so mean. She would have killed me if you didn't arrive." She smirks as she holds him. Markus stands there tempted to hug her. He remains there waiting for her to stop as his arms raise up out of his control. She breaks the hug. "Right. Well Morse is under my control. She will be of use." He would turn to see the city. One of the Legion officers would start up the helicopter. Markus watches the city. His eyes flash red before returning to blue. He would hold his head before heading to the helicopter with Buck and Reyes. Reyes holds her Wolf on the helicopter before it lifts off and heads back to the farm.

CHAPTER

15

QUEST OF POWER

Within the day of the burning of the Police station Markus would look out to see Police and Hunter agents move through the city. He orders all his men to pull out of the station. Buck looks at Markus. "Thought we were saving the station?" Markus remarks. "The station is lost. Let them have the ash. This city is ours to defend." They look out to the city. The station is still spewing large clouds of smoke. Every officer in the city rushed to the police station.

Within hours police, firefighters, and Hunter agents arrive at the Police station. As all three groups search for survivors they would find Amanda Morse and a few officers and agents. The police and firefighters rescue them as they try to save the building as well. After a while the police surround Amanda berating her with questions. "What happened? Where is the captain? Who did this?" Their questions go on as Amanda tries to calm them. "I can't answer all at once. We were attacked swiftly I... I don't remember what happened. Something hit me." They all would shake their heads. Amanda stands tall and takes command. "We need to protect this city and the people. Continue patrols and stay together. We are highly outnumbered, so call in all off duty cops." The police would get back to their cars and go on patrols to find the ones who destroyed their station and killed their friends. A few officers would stay with the station, attempting to bring certain equipment back on. Such a dispatch. While Amanda would take her Hunters and scout the city looking for Markus.

Legion members and Police aid the people of the city. Fighting each other at each corner. Throughout the week Police officers would disappear or become less interested in the Legion. Though, police would begin to gather at a police warehouse. Thornvel would stand on a box with the Police captain talking to the officers there. "I am Leia Thornvel and I have the truth. The Legion attacked our station. They had monsters, real demons, fighting alongside them. They turned our own against us. However, fear not. We still can beat them. They acted prematurely revealing themselves. We can expose them to the people and end them quickly. Free our City!" The officers would be inspired by her words as they cheer and clap. "We must remain in groups of six. Two police cruisers. If we can find the Legion members we can show them to the public and make them see that the people are not on their side. Show their own numbers they are criminals. Whether they like it or not. We can bring these crooks down just like any other criminals. Justice will be done!" They cheer the last words. "Justice will be done!" The Justice officers, as the police would refer to this group, became only interested in hunting the Legion, even those among their ranks. Soon the National Guard would arrive and declare Houston under Martial Law. Amanda Morse, Thornvel, the Police captain, and a young officer would meet in the remains of the police station. A soldier with a silver bar on his collar flaps would walk to them. He salutes the captain and Amanda. "Lieutenant Maximus. I have been called in by Governor Leathers. What is the situation?" Amanda would stand at her normal superior stance. "Well Lieutenant. A group of criminals attacked and severely destroyed this station. The support of the people is split. Some believe their crimes while others don't. My agents have been searching for traces or any details on Legion involvement. to prove it." Then Thornvel would speak up. "As the FBI investigates so the people turn in these monsters, the Police are having a hard time maintaining order. Though our focus should be on the Legion. They are taking crimes into their own hands. Still pretending to be vigilantes. They likely cause all these crimes they solve." Her anger would seep out. The lieutenant would take in all this info. "With martial law we will have easier control. We will arrest anyone after curfew. We will place checkpoints along all entry points. No one will slip past us." Thornvel looks to the Lieutenant. Her eyes show rage and sadness. "They have monsters in their ranks. Little demons I would advise to be careful. Very careful." The lieutenant looks to the captain who remained silent. "Your officer is not fit for work. Has she been resting?" The captain would sigh. "She is not lying. Some of our officers have seen the horror of the beasts. It is… devastating. They are pure evil." The lieutenant would not believe them. Scoffing at the idea. "I will get my men to their stations. I will also have patrols so hopefully we can restore order." He leaves the room. Thornvel scoffs and walks out in a huff. Her captain would look to Amanda. "Any intel on the Legion?" Amanda nods cleverly. "Yes I do. There is a Legion spot that my agents saw members of this gang enter. They seem to be there in mass. I suggest: shoot to kill." The Captain would nod, his eyes carrying a feeling of defeat. He sighs heavily, shaking his head. "Can we actually defeat them?" Amanda remains quiet. "I am not sure as of yet, but if we do this I can tell you what I think after." The captain nods and walks away. Amanda then smirks and contacts someone. "Morse here. Get the men ready. We have recruits."

Thornvel would sit at the entrance of the Police department. The captain walks over. "Lucas Gordon died right there, in that hall. He has been... had been my partner for so long. Wish we had more time. A lifetime." She holds back her tears as she curls up. The captain kneels down and places a hand on her shoulder. "Hold on to his memory. I am taking some officers to help the agents find the Legion. You are to help and organize the remaining officers." Thornvel jumps her head up and looks to the captain. "Captain, let me help. I can find them better than the FBI." The captain stands. "Those are my orders, Detective Thornvel." The captain would walk away as Thornvel stood up confused. She had the urge to go after him or investigate herself. However her emotions were mixed. Unable to decide what to do. Soon enough she would go to help the others capture their traitorous officers. Amanda Morse and a lot of Hunter Initiative agents would be rolling out to take out the Legion. Police would be mostly focused on upholding the peace in their city, thanks to martial law it makes it a bit easier, but each and every officer feels in their gut that it will only get harder. Amanda and her agents along with Police arrive at a warehouse in the outskirts of the city. They slowly move into the warehouse searching for their targets. It was dark and the power would not come on. After a few minutes each if the teams reach the middle and become confused. The captain would look for Amanda's team, but she was missing. The sound of boots hitting the metal deck overlooking the crates and officers below. The police and agents turn their guns and gaze upon the unknown man in terror. Markus would stop at a small broken window. "Gentlemen. Ladies. I am afraid you have been lured into a trap." Gremlin eyes open in the darkest corners of the warehouse surrounding the men and laughing. "I have no ill will towards any of you. The agents in your group though... I do not take kindly to crooks." The police look to the Agents. "The Hunter Initiative. Hunting down more than empowered criminals. But people of importance. From government officials to police chiefs. They bribe, blackmail, threaten, and hurt people to maintain the power of greed and tyrants. So my good officers. Will you join me in the cause to protect the people of this country? Or will you serve the corrupt, the criminals in power?" The words echo in their heads as they look at the Hunter agents. They, in return, look back at the officers. The captain and a few officers would not believe Markus. "You lie to deceive us, to turn us on one another. We have a warrant for your arrest... but we will certainly take your head instead." "He speaks the truth!" Amanda says walking out behind the group along with other Hunters, all the servants of Markus. The Gremlins and slaves move in to capture the police and agents. They force them to their knees in a line. Each struggle against their captors. Markus leans over the railing and lands on the first floor before walking over to the captured officers first. He would hold each hand to them. Most of them seem to distrust their "allies" of the FBI. They show signs of loyalty to their captors. Markus's words were echoing in their minds. They believed he was right and so joined him. The captain and a few other officers were neither guilty of greed or corruption or loyal. "They will be our prisoners." They take the Captain and his officers away. The Hunter agents begin to beg for their lives offering their loyalty. While some spoke truth, Markus would brand the others and leave the possible loyal hunters alone to think. "You all did crimes and criminal things to people. You are all guilty. Why should I take you as loyal servants? What is to stop you from doing more?" They swear to him they will not continue. Their words climb over each other attempting to gain their freedom, to hold their will. Shadow appears and whispers. "They have done many bad things. Perhaps we can see how loyal they can be?" Markus thinks for a moment. "No. My men fought against allowing crime. We will make the world better." Shadow would speak up "but master." Markus's red eyes appear as his voice becomes deeper, darker, as if it was another person speaking. "You will obey me! Crime is still crime." He brands them with the mark of chains.

Amanda returns with the enslaved and loyalists. Pretending to be defeated. They lost the captain and a few men. Days go by as Police search and capture Legion members whether within their ranks or outside it. However the Military started cracking down. They encircle food markets and check everyone. Criminals to ordinary citizens are detained. Causing people to fear or hate either the military or the Legion for causing it. The Hunter agents are nearly all under Markus as the Police are left divided. Trust was breaking between officers, anything suspicious would be reported and would result in detaining the officers. The police chief of Houston had been returning to the city. An old man with a white mustache and short buzz cut hair. He was in his police uniform speed walking towards the Military officers and burst into an officer meeting. "WHAT THE HELL HAS HAPPENED TO MY CITY!" He yells so loud it nearly frightened the soldiers and officers alike. The Lieutenant, Lieutenant Maximus, would speak calmly, yet with an agitated motion. "Your officers fight among themselves for traitors. Apparently this gang called the Legion of Darkness has crooked cops. Lots of them. Your station burns, your city is under martial law and worse off. The FBI is also here and failed to take down this gang." The chief would take out his phone. "The governor better have a reason for this!" After a small talk with the governor, the chief is sitting in a chair displeased. "Unbelievable... so the Legion became such a problem we had to call them in? Lieutenant Maximus, get the FBI out of my city. We don't want the Legion to take their gear." The Lieutenant responds. "Sorry sir, but they are searching for the Legion while we keep the peace. They are the only group not turning on one another." The chief scoffs as his foot taps the ground impatiently. "Fine, if I can get the Police organized will we pull the FBI out?" Lieutenant Maximus thinks, looking at the map of the city. "Maybe. If your officers can get organized and find more info than them. If you can do that. I will tell the FBI captain to get out." The chief stands up and moves to leave, he stops before walking out. "Oh. Tell them the Government has a breach. That will get them out." He walks out and towards a police SWAT van getting into the passenger side before it drives into the city. The chief arrives at the smoking ruins of their old police station. He would get out and take his hat off, closing his eyes and placing his hat to his heart. Honoring the dead. The chief then searches for Thornvel, who would be in charge of the Police remnants. He would find her on the roof looking at the city and the empty streets. The chief walks over to Thornvel. "Officer

Thornvel. Good to see you again." "Police Chief Wells. Good to
see you too. Been a while since I've seen a friendly face." "What
is wrong with all of our fellow officers?" Thronvel sighs and
would be unable to stop her eyes from tearing up. "Traitors are
within our ranks. We all eye each other. Trust is breaking faster
than glass shattering. We don't know if any more have joined
this Legion." The chief hugs her and tries to calm her down.
"The few officers we have should be trusted. I mean if they
were traitors they would have turned beforehand." Thronvel
would pull away after he said that. "You don't understand. The
Legion have monsters. They are fear itself, nothing we have seen
before. Demons that will bring us down." The chief crosses his
arms with doubt. "Thornvel you and the others must have seen
some terrible things. But there is no such thing as demons. Just
messed up people who act like them." "You don't understand…
not till you see them." The chief sighs and places a hand on her
shoulder. "You and some men will take some R and R to regain
your thoughts. I will take charge." Thornvel is worried as she
looks into Wells's eyes and begs him "no we need everyone
Chief. Please don't do this. We know what we saw and what
we are doing." "I will not have any of that Thornvel. Go cool
off. I am the Chief of Police in this city." Thornvel, saddened
by the stubborn nature of the chief, walks away and into the
office where Gordon and herself worked together. She would
cry sitting at Gordon's desk and curl up.

While Chief Wells reorganized many of the Police, he had
many who believed him mad to stop the hunt for the traitors
and Legion members. Like Thornvel, they were sent home

to cool off. It wouldn't be long before the remaining police would continue their patrols, being captured and sent back or killed. Lieutenant Maximus would notice the reorganization and keeping his word would track down Amanda Morse. He would find her and the other agents discussing how to corner the Legion within the city. As Maximus walks in he and some of his men get an unsettling feeling. A cold chill down their backs. Maximus clears his throat before speaking to Amanda. "Agent Morse. We request you and your agents leave the city. We have it under control now that the police are no longer hunting their own." Amanda smiles and then laughs. "You must be joking. The Legion is on the loose and is stronger than the Police." Maximus sighs before speaking up. "Chief Wells sends word the government is Breached." The words crawl into Amanda's brain as she opens her eyes surprised and regains her pose. "The Chief of Police said that? Very well." She informs her agents. "It is time." They begin packing up and getting all their equipment into the SUVs and trucks. Before they move out Amanda would ask the lieutenant. "Where is the chief? Perhaps we can give him all the data?"

Within the City Police patrol the streets and the Chief and some of his best officers stood at city hall which was being evacuated. "The government personnel need to be taken out of the city until this is resolved." The chief says he walks into the building with his officers and gathers everyone. He requests some armored SWAT trucks to help escort the mayor and others out. Instead the Hunter SUVs pull up and they move in behind Amanda. She nods to an officer standing outside. She walks towards the Chief. "Chief, you can not be serious about sending us away. Our mutual friend wanted us here." He glares at her. "It is because you are linked to the Governor. Your... branch can't be linked to this failure. You could not handle these common criminals. Hunters... you are a joke. Leathers should have requested my return for this." Before Amanda could say anything the lights started to glitch out. Then sudden gunfire is heard within the building. Screams and yelling heard and echoed in the mind of the chief. Soon the sounds would go silent. Only the footsteps of one man would get closer to the room Amanda and Wells were in. As the man enters they see Markus before them, before Wells could draw his gun Amanda drew hers and pointed it to his head. "What are you doing Morse!?" She smirks. "Serving my master. Now you hold files and information on Leathers. Don't you?" The chief would glare at them. "No, Governor Leathers has no record." Markus walks over. "Oh but he does. Everyone does. School, work, all hold records and police can access these files." "You can't have them, they are government documents." Markus looks at some books on a nearby shelf and then goes to the desk. "You can either deal with me... or my little monsters." The chief snickers. "I'm no fool, you have no real monsters. Not sure how you con-" before he could finish a few Gremlins leap onto his desk and laugh, sending Wells into a panic as he is in disbelief. "They are not real! They are not real!" Shadow stands on his shoulder and whispers "tell our master the truth." Wells is frozen in fear as his eyes slowly look over. His head moves shakingly over to see Shadow and the terrifying smile of sharp teeth. Wells falls to the floor fear engulfed him as he can't make sense of what he is seeing. Markus and Amanda walk out while Shadow and the gremlins have fun with their prey, his screams would be shut out by the doors closing. Within an hour the Chief is in cuffs and has this lifeless look as if he was consumed and spit out less of a man. Amanda would stand by him. "So with his passwords and information on the governor we can even use the corruption to end the control of the greedy. Meaning the military will stand down. The other states will still watch us." Markus would look out the window. "Get Reyes and Buck, with this evidence we can bring the people in and hide the attack on the Police station, instead blaming the HellHounds. This city is ours."

Hours later, news reporters and civilians arrive at the mayor's city hall. The mayor would be nervous with Amanda by his side. "Mayor, all you have to do is tell them everything is fine and let me do the rest." The mayor gulps and looks into the building. "You sure those um... men are not criminals?" She nods and stands at attention with her hands behind her back locked together. Her undoubting pose gives the mayor the motivation to go to the stand and speak to the public. "People of Houston. Our great city has long been a source of crime and greed. Sadly that greed did not stop at the underbelly. Captain Amanda Morse of the FBI was called to investigate. Captain." He moves from the podium as Amanda takes the spot. "Your mayor is correct. The Chief of Police, James Wells, was found purging data linking himself, the Governor and others to the HellHounds gang. They have used these criminals for personal gain. The chief had known that his friend and your governor, Edward Leathers, had hired gangsters to help with securing a seat in the government. The chief could have arrested the governor many times before but aided in his rise to power. But thanks to the Legion of Darkness, who fought the corruption, we found the evidence and data, though some erased, the Hellhounds led a false flag assault on the Police Station to make the Legion our enemy. Now the Legion will help rout out the corruption and bring your city into greatness! We thank their leader! Kronos!" Markus walks out of the main building with Buck and Reyes and her pet Waffles. They take the stage as people slowly begin cheering them on. Though they could see doubt lingered,yet trust in their government also began to fade. The military would be called off by the mayor and even the corrupt governor. Markus would stand with a grin. "This is our age, our time."

CHAPTER

16

SYMBOL OF THE PEOPLE

Within a few weeks the martial law is completely gone as people can walk and be outside. Thanks to the Legion finding the corrupted officials the lockdown was over and people praised them. While the city returned to normal, Police were still low in numbers and could not get every crime. The Legion stepped up and began protecting people. Arresting minor offenders and making a temporary jail for the Police. However major offenders like murderers and gangsters would be killed on sight. However some are arrested and brought to Markus. Markus, Reyes, Buck, and the loyal officers of the Legion had their own plans and would be given approval by Markus.

Markus and Amanda would stand atop the old Police building. "We shall rebuild this city for you my Lord. Starting with this poor excuse of a Police station." Amanda says, smirking. Markus would be thinking. Earlier he would be standing with Reyes and Buck hearing the speech from the Mayor and Amanda. Shadow would appear on his shoulder. "Master, I have found a new ability you can bestow on loyal servants. Even your infiltrator." Markus would look over at him. "Another power?" "No master, an extension. You can grant loyal servants the power to brand loyalists and brand criminals. No longer are you the source of recruitment." Markus would think on it as Reyes places a hand on his arm. "You can expand your idea to others and create a world wide force to keep peace. Nations would be able to work together and the people will seek to make their homes better." Even Buck speaks up. "This can let us expand our ranks and help the innocent. We can even truly see if someone is guilty of criminal acts instead of imprisoning innocents." Their words rattled in Markus's mind as he nodded. "I will think on it." Markus looks away from Shadow and out towards the city. He looks out for a moment and speaks up. "You will be my agent on the inside. The Hunters are useful, they can find all the dirty politicians and corrupt police and agents. All of your unit is mine, take them and enslave those who have done these monstrous acts you and your hunters have done." He looks at her with red eyes. "Give me the power to end all corruption!" Amanda bows as Markus raises his hands. "I Bestow you, my infiltrator slave, Amanda Morse, the power to spread my will and end the corruption." "Yes my Lord, your will shall be done." She stands, blessed by his powers, and leaves to take her agents back to their HQ.

While Markus would bestow this on Reyes, Buck, Jones, and Greg. His loyalists patrolled the city hunting criminals and helping the people to the best of their abilities. Buck led the Legion forces in hunting HellHounds and criminals. Buck would only enslave those who he viewed as irredeemable and those who proved their loyalty he welcomed with open arms. Boosting public approval of the Legion. Buck would run into some trouble with some Police who tried to warn the people. A few police stood out in a park with red paint on their shoulders and white paint going down their back like a line. "People of Houston. The Legion are deceiving you! They speak of justice and helping, but they killed many police and turned many others to serve their needs! They may do the same to you! Be a thorn in the side of injustice!" Buck and a few Legion members walk over. "Enough you are scaring people with lies. Most of your officers willingly joined. Others were greedy and corrupted and are now removed from their corruption." The rebel police step down and get in their faces. "You are nothing but criminals. You execute any who commits a crime. There is no justice in killing everyone. Where are the trials, where are the facts? You are not judge, jury and executor." Some people agree with the police while the others boo them. "The Legion finally drew out corruption." One says as another agrees. "That is right! We suffered under the HellHounds too!" The police rebels would shake their heads. "The Legion are not heroes, they will take what they want like any crook. Your choices are to either leave the city or help us end their rule early!" Buck would walk over to the center. "I am Buck Layne, I was once an unfortunate soul who was part of the HellHounds. Lord Kronos spared me and I realized that there was someone willing to stop the HellHounds who took everything. Our lives, our money. I took a loan from the wrong people. Some of you know what I mean, the HellHounds force anything to get their payment back. Now we have a chance to end the drug trafficking, human trafficking, and killings." The people cheer him on. He turns to the police Rebels who leave in disgust. Buck and his Knights move on, but are stopped by a few young men and women who want to join to make the world better. Buck smiles and tells them how dangerous it can be and that they should focus on getting a job. Some listened but others still wanted to join. So he would take them to the Police station and show them the power of Kronos. Reyes would look at the new recruits as she was taking some slaves for her club. Instead she gets an idea.

Reyes goes to her old club and opens it to the homeless or those in trouble. Within weeks she would get many people seeking help and food. She asked Markus in person to come see and help the people. As she would sit in her old throne Markus walks over. "And how does this help people?" Reyes laughs and stands up taking his arm gently. "This doesn't, the food and your slaves help a little. Look at them. They have lost hope and have nowhere to go. Most lost homes or are ex HellHounds who were forced to leave their old lives for the gangsters. But if you want to help them. Give them hope, a power to see and worship." "I am not a god, Reyes. I am a man just like them." She brings him downstairs. "Your powers say otherwise. Let me show them. Show them the healing power you have, show them the power over death you have. This will inspire them. You are a Titan who can save this world." Her words slithered into his mind, her venomous words convinced him. Her goal was pure. Support the man she had fallen for. "I just want to help, money is no problem, but all that will be used for our people. Your people, Kronos." Markus nods and walks to the center of the room. "Very well." She smirks and takes out a revolver. The people look over and see Kronos. Among them was Rebecca, the wife of jones. Reyes would stand by him. "This is Lord Kronos, leader of the Legion of Darkness and has been supplying us with the chefs and food here. He is powerful and will do everything to ensure you survive. With his power, this titan, he will ensure you all are fed and cared for." The people would doubt it. "We thank you for the food sir, but it does not mean you are some god. Not a Titan either." An old man says. Rebecca walks over, She would turn to the people. "What she says is true.

Science could not heal me, some of you know me and know the condition I was in. Lord Kronos gave me a Miracle. He saved my life and saved my children from living without a mother. Nani, come here." a Woman limps over to Rebecca, she had blonde hair and would be in a state of despair. "Nani here has a tumor and cancer, she also broke her leg in a crash and it was never fully healed. Show them your power my lord." He uses the life of some of his Gremlins to cure the woman. She yells in pain as a loud crack sounds and she looks around. She would walk normally and be swimming in happiness. She was cured and everyone was in amazement, some even got on their knees and bow. A few stood there and mocked them. "She is a paid actor. This is bullshit. Gods are not real." Reyes would hold up a bullet. "This is a real bullet, does anyone want to test if it is real?" The boy walks over and examines it. "Yeah, real enough to kill anyone." She loads it into a revolver and shoots Markus. Everyone is surprised and screams, shocked that she killed Kronos. Within seconds he stands up and takes a bullet out of his chest. They all are shocked and even the boy gets on his knees. Markus walks over to the boy and Reyes slowly. The boy begins to beg. "I didn't know my lord, I swear. By your name I swear. Lord Kronos, have mercy!" Markus looks at Reyes, who smirks. She hands him the gun and helps the young man up. "Worry not, He has mercy on all who do no harm unless in the name of Justice." Everyone looks up or straight at Kronos. He would look at them all. A sigh of hope in their eyes, and fear in others. He speaks boldly and firmly. "If you have done harm, fear not. Redeem yourselves by helping others. Give yourselves to your neighbors and friends. Aid this city and report all crime.

The only crimes that are unforgivable are killing and corrupting others. Do not let greed or power blind you and you will be spared!" he would then walk back upstairs. As he walks away they all chant his name. "Hail Kronos the Titan god! Kronos! Kronos!"

Jones would later hear of Kronos's appearance at the Kings of Pleasure club and how he inspired people. His wife, Rebecca, tells him of what happened and that people joined a nightly prayer to Kronos, to grant him strength and power to end the Crime in Houston. They call themselves the Titan's Creed. Jones would be happy for his wife and grateful she lives. He would think of a way to honor Kronos. Weeks later he would come up to Kronos at the Farm. He takes a knee and lowers his head. "Lord Kronos, may I make a request?" Markus would be looking at a map of the city then turn to him. "You may rise Jones, no need to kneel before me. What is it?" Jones rises. "My Lord you are gaining followers and support fast, even the religion that just formed called the Titan's Creed." "Ah yes the Creed. Reyes is leading it as... what did she say it was? Oh right as the Enlightened Speaker. Your wife is her second, holding the title of... I believe it was the First Blessed." Jones nods and places his hands behind his back and stands tall. "You are the reason for my wife's life, I wish to repay you with loyalty and I wish to request you to be your Guard. In the future I will be your guard captain until someone of greater skill is-" Markus holds his hand up to quiet him. He then goes over to a chest and opens it pulling out a Katana. "I love the blades of Spartans, even the knights. But the Japanese Blade spoke to me. While the Blade of a Spartan was one of Glory, a knight was one of justice. This blade has always been a symbol of Honor, even Loyalty. Take this blade and keep it at your side. Show me the Loyalty you wish to give me. Honor me with your blade and gun. Defend me with honor, fight for me with Loyalty." Markus brings the sword over to Jones. "This sword is the embodiment of Honor and Loyalty. Will you hold this blade, honorbound to fight in my name? Will you uphold your loyalty? This blade will decide. The day you forget your honor and the day you abandon your loyalties, this blade will be your end." Jones reached for the hilt of the blade, the weight of the duty would be heavy. His fingers slowly wrap around the hilt of the sword, his life now bound to this blade and to his friend and leader. Markus let's go of the katana and places a hand on his shoulder. "Confidence, that is good my friend. Now go enjoy your day and tomorrow, dawn your new armor." Jones would be surprised as he bows and takes his new katana with honor and pride returning home. The next morning Jones stands by Markus's side in his new armor. Black leather armor fitted to his chest, the symbol of a white sword pointing up in the middle. His arms bear Heavy Leather armbands and a leather pauldron on his left shoulder. Under his pauldron is a long black cape with an outline of white. The cape covers his left arm hiding the pistol and most of the katana. The cape also bears the flag of the Legion of Darkness. Jones stood proudly in his armor. "My lord, how did you make this?" Markus would smile under his mask and sit at the window. "Well one of our loyalists was a professional costume maker. She was really good at it before her kidnapping. Now she makes most of our leather armor. She wants to try some metal which I will save for Buck and Greg. Maybe I can have her make new blades." Jones would look out the window. "We would be honored to wear these gifts, Lord Kronos." Markus would remove his mask and sit back in his chair. "My old name was Markus. Doubt I will be using it for a long time." Jones would be shocked. "Do the others know?" "No, I plan on sharing this with Buck when he gets his blade too. As my Blight Commander he should know." Jones would check his face. "You look pretty young, Cursed with youth?" He says jokingly. "Cursed to never die I guess. My first death was... I am not sure how long ago. A year or less? Cerberus, the Leader of these gangsters, killed me by snapping my neck. He seemed to like the name I gave him." Jones is surprised. Markus would then put his mask on and stand, before someone knocked on the door. Markus and Jones would continue the week managing important matters.

North of Texas into South Dakota, a small building in the middle of nowhere with a helicopter pad on top. Inside Amanda would stand before a few Hunter officers. "Your mission was to stop the Legion and aid Governor Leathers keep the masses calm. Instead you aid the targets and cause one of our assets to become a target of blame and public questioning." Amanda would look confident. "Sir, the Legion can give us better support than the Governor. He worked sloppily and was often caught. His friend, the police Chief, had to bail him out of being seen in public. They were a weak asset." The Officers were sitting in the dark, there were nine of them. "What can a bunch of vigilantes do? They will cause more problems than help." Amanda smirks and steps forward. "Exactly. If the Legion continues to gain people's support, they will be targeted by our other assets. Our Assets will do anything to keep their power. We can use that to send the perfect candidate for President forward. If they want the Legion gone, then next election they will boost our perfect candidate and make them amazing in the eyes of the people." The officers are impressed. The idea brings a dark smile to their hidden faces. One of them speaks. "This Idea might get you into the Council. A tenth member would be interesting." Amanda would smile.

Nearly a month passed by after Jones became the Bodyguard of Kronos, the reconstruction of the Police Station would be nearly complete. Legion Police members Would stand at a ceremony with the Mayor. He opens the Police Station, though for now it is Only able to hold an armory and the offices of the Police, however a few jail cells are still being built. Markus, Reyes, Buck, Jones, and Greg were all in the station while the ceremony continued. They held the previous Chief in a cell, muttering and broken. Buck would look at the chief feeling a little bad. "I would rather be a slave than a broken man." Greg would check him. "I say we end him, he has no use like this. To anyone." Markus would stare at the man. "Perhaps you are right Greg. We can leave him to Shadow and the gremlins. Only right they should end the mess they made." Reyes walks over to Markus. "My Lord, why not make him an example instead?" Jones looks confused and speaks up. "What example? What do you mean?" She looks over to Jones and smiles. "An example of what corruption will lead to. Let the world know that when there is corruption the unjust will be destroyed in their own darkness." Markus looked at the husk of a man, his blue eyes looking with sorrow. "We are not monsters, he is a husk. Give the soul rest. Give his body to the gremlins." Buck nods and opens the cell pulling out a dagger and holding Wells's shoulder. "Rest in peace, may your soul find redemption." He thrusts his dagger into the chief's heart. Wells takes a breath and looks up at Buck and passes on. The group would wait for a while before Shadow and some gremlins drag the body into a shadow, disappearing. The group would then walk up stairs for an office to speak in. The police would bow to Markus as he walked by. Once in the room they discuss tactics and plans. Markus would begin. "So tell me what you all have done? What plans are you doing and wish to put forth?" The group sits in chairs around a rectangular table. Reyes on the left, Jones on the right, while Buck and Greg sit across from Markus. Reyes would soon stand up. "The plan for the Titan's Creed is simple. Establish a new religion. Creating devoted believers and future warriors. These devotees can also help the common people and spread good will and your name. As for my clubs, they can be places for VIPs and important men and women can go to reveal details. My ladies are already preparing to serve my lord." Markus would put his hand against his mask where his lips would be, thinking. "Not a bad idea. The Legion can make money for the people and for our cause. Make sure the VIP stuff is pricey and directed to company executives and government officials. Oh and give the police a discount. See if we can lure in some of those rogue Police." She nods with a smile and sits down. Buck stands. "Speaking of the Rogue Police, they are attempting to rally the people to their cause. But with our Legion Police and

Legion knights, we are pulling more people to our side." Greg stands with Buck. "Hunting the criminal organizations has been easy. We have even given them chances at surrender. Most do take it, the few that don't await your judgment." Markus chimes in. "And of those you allowed to surrender?" Greg smiles. "We are currently putting them in community service. They are now working as construction workers, picking up trash and becoming contributing civilians." Markus nods. "Well done you two and of the HellHounds?" Buck sighs. "Since the Hunter Initiative and Police interfered they have had time to hide their tracks and keep hidden. It could be that they disbanded, but I doubt it." "Keep searching. Cerberus is not one to end his gang. I am more interested in his professional criminal group. His elites." They nod and sit. Jones would stand. "I actually looked into the Police database. It seems that the leader is not known to them, even the Chief's computer had nothing." "No worries Jones. As for our Police unit. I believe Jones here should be their commander. They will report to him and can act as Police Commander in the worst case scenario." The others nod and agree. "Buck you will be my Blight Knight Commander." "Why Blight? Doesn't that sound a bit dark." Markus chuckles. "We are the Legion of Darkness. You will bring a Blight to the corrupted lands and once the blight claims these lands, they can heal and be lands of light." Buck would not like the name, but agrees to being his Blight Commander. Markus and the others stand and leave the Police station. "There is much work to be done. Inform me when we find the HellHounds." His eyes turn red. "They shall crumble and this city will be free of three headed mutts.

CHAPTER

17

NEW DREAMS

Markus stands atop the farmhouse, now looking more like a fort with walls being constructed. He would think back on all that happened. He would think about who he is becoming, who he is. The HellHounds are quiet, the military gone, the Hunters enslaved, and the government leaving the Legion alone. The silence gave Markus some time to think. He would drop off the edge and turn a full 180 grabbing the ledge and swinging into the window below him. He would sit at the table in the room. After a bit he hears a light knock on his door. "Come in." Reyes walks in with her pet wolf, Waffles, she would stand at the window closing it. "Lord Kronos. I know you are eager to finish this war, but I figured some relaxation is needed. Don't want our lord tired." "I can be out there searching too, Miss Tonka." Reyes would sit across from him. While Waffles lay down under the middle of the table. His head facing Reyes's legs. "You could, but no. We need you to wait for Cerberus to make himself known. If they know you are personally hunting him, they may stay hidden for a long time." Markus would think about what she said. As she continues to talk he listens closely. "You are the soul and master of this Legion. You will change the world and bring a new age to humanity." She holds one of his hands softly. "You are powerful and use that power for the world. Such power can change the world, Kronos." Markus would sigh. "My name is… or was Markus." he takes his mask off. "I was killed to get this power. I died for power. Sure I have the ability to make the world better. But-" she stands up and walks over to Markus. "You are Kronos now. As Markus you were a boy who gave his life in defense of others. Now you are Kronos. Lord of the shadows, Liberator of the people. Master of

monsters and men. Do not stay in the past, look to the future."
Markus's eyes turn red for only a moment. Reyes would see
this and move closer to Markus. "You are the Future. Let go
of the past. Become Kronos and Lead humanity to a new age.
A age of Unity." She would move away and slowly walk out of
the room. "Trust in me, trust in your Gremlin, trust in your
power." She closes the door as Markus looks at the table and
holds his mask. He would wait an hour before putting it back
on and walking out.

Riding in a Blue truck heading down to the Police station,
Markus had his mask off with Jones driving. It was quiet for a
while before Markus spoke up. "How do you feel about where
I am taking the Legion? The Religion of me, the enslaving, the
killing?" Jones would be silent for a moment. Focused on the
road and then stopping at a restaurant. "My Lord, Look at that
place. Before you I wanted to come here, but it was covered with
HellHounds and Drug dealers. Now look at it." The people at
the place were having fun, enjoying their meals and talking as
if nothing bad could happen. It would bring a smile to Markus's
face. "You did that My lord. If not for your strength to fight
and kill, even being merciful at times, This restaurant would be
closed. Most would worry about more shootings and killings.
Without you, the city would be lost and the HellHounds would
rule." Markus would look out at the city as they continued the
drive. They would arrive at the Station. Markus puts his mask
on and walks up to the doors. Two Police would bow and open
the door for Markus. Markus nods and walks into the Station
looking for Buck. After a bit he would meet with Buck in the

Old Captain room, with no windows and a large table with a map of the city. While Jones stood guard at the door for a private talk, Markus would walk towards Buck, who bowed. "Lord Kronos, Been a while." Markus would nod. "It has. No need to bow in private. I have some things to discuss." Buck would stand straight and look to his Lord with pride. "Of course my Lord." "First I wish to know your thoughts on our actions. My actions." Buck would look down then sigh. "My thoughts are the same as many of our men. The HellHounds and city left many of us to suffer and die in the back alleys. The fight against such a way required killing. Though I am not always for enslaving any rule breakers. Murders and worse, sure. However your choices lead to where we are now. The city has had little to no crime. The HellHounds are too scared and some believe they abandoned the gang to try and survive our blade." "In other words you believe I have done right?" Buck nods and looks over the map. "Quite a few of your men were under the influence of drugs or forced into loans, you cured the afflicted and ended our debt. Many of us would suffer without your choices." Markus smiles a bit more under his mask. Markus would remove his mask and Tell Buck his story, how he was Markus and had died. Yet Buck didn't care. "My lord, you are Kronos now. Markus is still part of you, his dreams and goals are within you. Now that you have the power to achieve them, a new goal, a new dream is needed for Kronos. Something that Kronos and his Legion can do." Markus laughs and then knocks on the door bringing Jones in with an extra sword. "Jones figured you would say about as much. While Jones is my bodyguard, carrying the blade of honor and loyalty. You shall carry the blade of glory and valor."

He pulls out a Spartan Sword. "A blade of a warrior, a fighter, a leader. Carry this blade and you shall earn Glory and hold up your valor. Command my Legion and show all who oppose Justice your blade. So long as you uphold your valor this blade will be your will. Fail and you shall find it shatter before you." Buck would hover his hand over the hilt. Focused on the blade admiring it and finally taking the hilt in an iron grip. "I Shall not fail you my Lord." Markus nods as Jones walks back out. "I will await your next report. As your Lord, Kronos." Buck would bow to Markus, as he leaves the room. Markus would head back to the fort his men were constructing, but it still weighed on him. Who he is, what he has done and most importantly what he will do. After returning to the farm Markus would retire to his room and rest.

Markus would be standing in the white room once more. The blood was half way to his legs. The statues look as if they were to crumble. He looks to the mirror on the other side of the room. There stood his other self. Still standing tall and mighty as if expecting him. Markus walks over to him. "Who are you?" Kronos laughs. "Forgot me already!? You have tried so hard to suppress me! But you know as well as I that you need me! Just as I need you. We are one coin, but two faces fighting for control over a small raft!" the Statues on the other side of the mirror would turn to face Markus. Markus would stumble back. "No, this is all wrong. I… I have not lost myself, I do not need you!" Kronos would reach for Markus. His arm goes through the mirror and grabs Markus pulling him against the mirror. "You might think that, but you have been in doubt this entire time!

You froze and I took control! Then you stop me and make our resolve weak!" Kronos lets go of Markus and backs up. "You are not a Lord or a ruler, you are a man of the people... though I do not partake in such kind gestures it does rally the people to a good leader. But you can not rule or win this war! You want to unite the world? Why not through justice! Through our power! I will offer this once Markus Mars. I, Kronos who holds no name, Offer you a truce. Let me take charge and lead us to a united world. We can not let greed and hate rule this world. Let me show you. Give me control." He pushes his hand through the mirror again and offers a handshake. Markus hesitates as he thinks. He reaches but pulls away before sealing the deal. "NO! I will be in control. There is already too much death. There are many good people. My parents, my friends, even my Legion. I will not let the flames of war burn." Kronos pulls his hand back and walks over to a throne forming. He sits and leans on one of his hands. "Then by all means do what you believe is right. But when the time comes where you are moments from losing yourself entirely I shall save you and keep you standing." He laughs, slowly getting louder. Suddenly Markus wakes. Sweeting and yet cold. He takes a moment to breathe before looking out the window and into the world. "I will unite people under a just and kind banner."

CHAPTER

18

BREACHING HELL

Weeks of searching brought nothing, but the Legion was determined and the HellHounds were becoming aggravated. The City would be busy with laughs, freedom and no worries for thugs or major crime. Some small thefts. Often a smack on the hand while the Legion continued to keep order. People would grow to love the Legion. Recruitment would be high, yet they would be careful who joins. Buck, Jones, even Reyes would be personally given the power of Branding. Buck would give his power to his top three men including Greg. Allowing the Legion to grow. Jones would conduct branding Prisoners who broke major rules, killing, rape, hurting people through drug dealing, enslaving people, and more. With the power of the Branding they would see if people were truly guilty. With Reyes She would Continue to grow the Titan's Creed. An order of women and men who would worship the power of Kronos and help others.

Meanwhile In the last true stronghold of the HellHounds. Cerberus and his most faithful and elite members would be preparing for their comeback. All they needed was a clean shot to the heart of the Legion of Darkness. Cerberus was sitting in his office thinking, furious that his plans were drowning. Looking out towards the city he once held with an iron grip. "To hell with this city. We will find another and regrow. One day we will take this city back. If only we had their home. Their leader." His fists clenched, his eyes filled with fire, his rage was overwhelming. His phone would ring within his suit. He calms down as he reaches for it. He answers the phone with a calm voice. "Hello?" The voice on the other side was low yet stern.

"The FBI went to a Farmhouse in the Northeast part of the city. It is an abandoned area, the only reason I am helping is because you are part of the Five." "Thank you, do not worry Mr.-" the caller hangs up before Cerberus could finish. Cerberus would stand up, his rage returning. He walks out of his office and grabs his heist mask walking out to get most of his crew. "Listen up! Those Legion bastards took what was ours! They crippled our business and barged into our turf. They took what is mine! What is yours! Now we have the chance to take it back. Pack your gear! We will attack from the air! Those who partake in the dirty work of the HellHounds, hold this building, you will all be rewarded for staying loyal as the next Elite Hounds." He would walk down the stairs to the crew that prepares. "You two." He points to a few gangsters. "Go find this farm the fools are based in. Send some pics and where it is. Do this and you two will be officers in the crew." The two look at each other and smirk. They rush off to the cars below. The rest of the crew get some high grade weapons, LMGs, MP5s, AR-15s, and even a few RPGs. They would all load them in large crates and move down to the car lot below the building. Getting the equipment into their vehicles and moving out to the airport.

A few Legion boys were nearby the penthouse of the HellHounds and saw the large convoy of black SUVs. Curiously they would call this in and have a few police cars, undercover police cars, even Legion cars. They switch back and forth to keep an eye until they reach the Airport. A few Legion members would be meeting a few friends within the Airport security. He would spot the cars and then sees them driving into the strip where a few helicopters are. He would watch them closely and would see the HellHound logo on a few of their backs as they got out. They finally found the HellHounds. Legion members would enter the hotel and walk up to the clerk. "Hello, we are interested in knowing who is in the Penthouse." The woman stands there with a forced smile. "I am sorry, but we can not give our client information." The men would look at each other. "Would a warrant help break your silence?" "I am sorry, we have a contract to not say who is staying at our hotel and Penthouse. If you are interested please take this pamphlet." She offers a pamphlet with her smile. One of the men takes it and walks out with his partner. They walk out of the building and into their car before looking into the pamphlet. It had a message inside it. "HellHounds hold Penthouse, holding staff hostage, families within the Hotel too. Please help." The men are shocked and drive quickly to the Police station where Buck and Greg were talking about going to the coastline. "It is likely the HellHounds are within other cities and left-" the door opens. "Commander, we found them!" Buck looks over and eagerly asks. "Where? Where are they held up? Do you know how many?" The man takes a breather. "Unsure, but they are in a penthouse in the Lucky Den." Buck would look at Greg. "get the boys. We are gonna end them today." Greg nods and walks out to gather the men. They all get some Police issued AR-15s and 12-Gauges, along with Glock 17s. Buck walks out to them as they put on Kevlar body armor and load some ammo into magazines. "Alright boys. Today some of our guys found some HellHounds leaving a hotel building. They investigated and found the idiots camping out in the penthouse. Now we are gonna finish them!

We will enter quietly and take out the guards before busting in and killing them. We find their boss, capture him and bring him to Lord Kronos after. You boys ready!?" The men nod in excitement. Adrenaline hitting them hard as they see the end of the HellHounds. They grab their guns and gear. Holding their guns in the air and yelling "For Lord Kronos! For the people! For the Legion!" Buck would smile and be filled with pride and raise his hand to the chant. They all get into their vehicles outside and drive to the towering building. As they move into the building, they take out the cameras and move to the elevators. The clerk would hide under her desk and stay quiet. Their confidence and excitement made the legion cocky. The realization that their war is almost over closes in on them as twenty men wait in the elevators. Their eagerness turns into tension. They lose their smiles and it clicks in their heads. They were walking into the lion's den. Their lack of caution and planning has their heads only an inch from the Lion's jaw. As they reach the penthouse the elevator ding goes off, but in their heads it was the bells of Hell. As the doors open their hearts are filled with adrenaline as Buck sees a single HellHound guard smoking. Buck lifts his heavy shotgun, as soon as the stock hits his shoulder the guard would drop his cigarette and pull out his pistol. He was too late as Buck pulls the trigger and unloads his shot into the guard's chest. The sound of the shot echos in the penthouse. The shock wears off as Buck and his knights move into the first room and keep their guns up. A few HellHounds burst into the room, but are gunned down instantly. The Legion regained their composure and kept their guns up. Trained on the doors, they would be refocused. Though their entrance left little preparation for the next part. On the other side of the doors the HellHounds would take up defensive positions. "Who the fuck dared to enter?" Buck and Greg would look at each other as they threw in a flash grenade. The Hellhounds are surprised. The few professionals would take cover as the less experienced criminals are flashed. While no one could hear anything for a while, the Knights would rush their position and use Shotguns for those rushing. A few stayed back and used the ARs for covering fire. The seconds of combat would be deafened by the ringing of the flashbang as Buck and his men shot and killed the HellHounds. Some of the criminals would be tackled and knocked out. As they reach the professionals, one of them takes their pistol and shoots one of the Knights in the shoulder. With the ringing dampening Buck only noticed his knight being shot out of the corner of his eye and then rolled past the professionals and pumped them full of lead. A few HellHounds come from the main room and shoot at the Knights and kill one of them. "Fuck! Dan!" Greg yells as he fires his AR at the HellHounds who are forced back into the main room. The Knights take up cover and suppress the main door. Buck would get up and take the wounded Knight back and give him to one of the others who tried to tend to his wound. "Dan is dead... Keep Kevin alive." The Knight nods and Buck returns to the shoot out. In the back he sees them carrying a large gun over to it. "Is that... a LMG?" buck says confused. "It is an AAI LSAT. Military made LMG." Greg said as he shot the man with the LMG. Missing his shot the HellHound heavy would unload into the hallway. The spray of hellfire would hit a few Knights who were trying to shoot back. Three men went down. Buck yells to Greg. "We need to take that bastard out!" Greg nods to Buck as he peaks out on one side of the hallway and takes a few shots at the gunner getting his attention. Buck then steps out and lines his shot up to the gunner and unloads a shot into the gunner's chest. The HellHound gunner drops to the ground with a loud thud as the other HellHounds reel back with a shocked expression. "He is a hell of a shot!" One of them yells as they pull back to the upper level, Cerberus' office. The dark knights move in and poorly secure the rest of the penthouse tossing furniture and keeping their eyes fixed on the door to the office. Greg would take two men and look around other rooms in the penthouse. Meanwhile Buck walks over to the door. "Come on out dogs, your gang is ending. You might as well be strays." One of the men on the other side yelled through the door, though muffled a little. "Go to hell bastards." The Knights laugh as Buck shakes his head. "Surrender now and we will just jail you. Until the strays of the old Hounds are either dead, captured, or dealt with in other manners. If we have to bust in there we are giving you to Lord Kronos." "Cerberus will have his head!" "Yeah the boss will get him!" The HellHounds sound confident and challenge the Legion with defiance. Greg would take a few of the Legion knights and go up on the roof while Buck gives their enemy the chance to live. "We outnumber you, we out-power you, we have the city, we are the police, the common people. Surrender and Lord Kronos may pardon you." The Hellhounds in the other room, all eight, remain still. Their sweaty palms, shaky hands, and heavy breathing is obvious to themselves. Their minds filled with regret and questioning their loyalty. Only two seem to be hopeful their boss will win. "Come take us then! We will kill you all. The boss will break your Lord Kronos. We are hell!" Greg and his squad secure some rope and jump over the edge of the building before shooting into the windows and crashing into them. One of the Knights rolls in with a shotgun and fires at the first armed HellHound. The other six drop their guns and drop to the ground while the last of the two loyal HellHounds grits his teeth and aims for the Knights. His reaction was too slow as Greg shoots the man as he swings in. The HellHounds cower before the Legion. Begging for their lives. Greg opens the door for Buck and the rest of the Knights. Cuffing the HellHounds who surrendered. Greg and Buck walk to the broken windows. "Can't believe that worked." Greg says with relief. "I can. You think their boss is really going for Kronos?" They look at each other before grinning. "Even if he did. He will not make it. Today is the end of the HellHounds" They look over the city, the city they have freed, the City that supports Kronos, the city that belongs to the Legion.

CHAPTER

19

UNLEASHED

During the assault on the HellHounds penthouse, Cerberus leads the last of his men. Composed of his elitists and a few gangsters. A helicopter would be flying over to the new fort of Kronos with a convoy of SUVs below on the road. Cerberus would be determined to take out Kronos and crush the Legion's leader. In the helicopter he looks at a few military grade LMGs in the middle of the chopper. Cerberus bellows his rage to his men. "These are thanks to our partners. Use them to show those fools we own this city!" The helicopter leaves the convoy going to the East while the Convoy leans more towards the West. Cerberus stares out into the open field in anger and discontent. His desire to reclaim what was his. Yet a muffled scream from within reaches his mind. Telling him to turn back. To leave. To go into hiding. All he does is grit his teeth, angered with whatever is telling him this. "I will not lose my power." He mutters to himself.

Meanwhile at the fort the underground construction goes well as they start moving in large supplies of wood to ensure their tunnels stay in position. The Slaves working most of it. But even the knights would help believing they are safe. Talking amongst each other. Even Kronos relaxes within the farm house, with Tonka and her pet Waffles. "This house is a nice place. I feel a bit bad for making it into a fort. Maybe we are done with this all." Markus says as he takes his mask off and sits across from Tonka. "My Lord, I am sure the world will still need you. Perhaps the criminal underworld can be destroyed. Or controlled. You could use the underworld to get information on major criminals." Markus laughs. "That is a good idea for a time.

However, to find whoever has big ties within the underworld will take many years. I am sure there is a structure even for the underworld. A secured structure. The Black Market, Black Web, even criminal run businesses. These are all covered in darkness. Even the light cannot shine onto them." Tonka would be petting Waffles with a smirk. "But the Darkness is our area. Isn't it?" Shadow would appear and walk over to Markus "Indeed master. If you so command it we could hunt for them. Your Gremlins can find them and destroy them. Freeing the world of such corruption." Markus would think about it. Believing that his curse could do more for the world than he thought. He put down a large gang that terrorized his city. Then it spread into other cities and now this gang is ashes in the flames of the Legion. "Perhaps you are both right. If we wish to spread the Legion and free this world then we should get a structure going. Perhaps Greg can help there. He is better with command structures. While talking, the watchtower at the edge of the fort spots the convoy of SUVs, radioing it in. "Farmhouse this is Southeast tower. I spotted a few SUVs all the same design about seven or eight. Request alert level 3." As he watches the SUVs they turn off the road and drive over the open land towards the fort. The watcher would be surprised and radios it in. While he does a HellHound pops out of the top window with a RPG firing at the tower. "Cancel that! The SUVs are attac-" The rocket hits the tower killing the man and sending it down in flames crushing a part of the wall they made for the farmhouse. The HellHounds move toward the South gate. Kronos and the rest of the fort hear the explosion. Kronos puts his mask on and looks out the East window to see what is going on. "An attack?

By the government? CIA? FBI? Maybe those Hunters?" He rushes downstairs and moves outside towards the South to see what comes through the gate. The SUVs run through their makeshift gate and stop at the edge of the walls, HellHounds getting out of the cars and moving towards the house with military grade weaponry. Kronos would glare at them with disgust, yet he held a bit of joy. Knowing they are on their last legs. He could crush them himself. "Legion! The enemy has broken through the gate! Defend your fellow knights. Fight for the liberty of Houston, for Texas!" The Legion slaves and loyalists arm themselves and rush to cover, unloading their bullets into the HellHounds. A gun fight rages on in the middle of the Legion fort, many of the Legion members were afraid. They did not believe they would be in combat, joining to be part of something. Kronos would draw a pistol and walk towards the battle. "The enemy has come to us! Stand up my knights! Show them the blade of justice! Show them the fangs of the Legion!" He raises his left hand, the sword symbol on his hand glows bright. The symbols on those who joined the Legion would glow as well as they get a boost of confidence and a type of adrenaline rush that pulls them out of cover and firing at the HellHounds with relentless fury. Markus would rush to cover behind a large haystack before drawing his other pistol and shooting the HellHounds with his men. The HellHounds lower their heads and upper body as they run to cover behind either their vehicles, farm equipment or stacks of wood planks. A few would fire their weapons from their hips suppressing a few Legion slaves and loyalists. A few from the wall rush through the tall wheat field. Seeing the HellHounds they either kneel down or drop to the floor and fire at the HellHounds. The few hip firing HellHounds are shot and killed while a HellHound professional throws a molotov into the wheat field burning the wheat. But the fire hits the two in the wheat as they run out and drop into the dirt ground as they scream for the flames to stop. A few others would try to put the fire out with a few buckets of water, yet too late to save their friends. "Fucking HellHounds!" They drop the buckets and pick their weapons up furious with the loss of their friends as they fired their ARs and shotguns. A few bolt rifles would be handed out at the house to allow long range shooting. The HellHounds would be pretty pinned as they lose a few unlucky men from the riflemen further away. The HellHounds situation is dim as the Legion keeps them suppressed with superior numbers. Then Cerberus' helicopter zooms over towards the battle. They sit on the floor of the helicopter and use LMGs firing down at the farmhouse killing a few Legion members who were picking off his men. Markus looks up at the helicopter. "Cerberus. Shoot the engines!" The Legion shoots up at the helicopter, their bullets either bouncing off the helicopter or barely denting it as Cerberus and his crew gun down nearly a dozen Legion members. The HellHounds at the gate would move up to attack the Legion with full force. However a few of them are shot with shotguns or AR-15s, both sides suffering losses. Markus' eyes turn red as he speaks to his gremlins. "Kill them, but bring Cerberus and his two officers to me. Just make sure my knights survive. Your Master demands it." The gremlins laugh as they appear from the shadows of items they sneak around the area catching a few HellHounds off guard as they leap onto them and pull them into the fields of wheat. Screams soon followed. The others would be confused as they hear the screams. "Alex? Elijah?" One of the HellHounds yells out before seeing yellow eyes in the wheat fields. He freaks out and unloads all of his ammo into the field. The others notice this and do the same, giving the Knights reason to move up and shoot them or surround them and force them into surrender. A few bullets would be chipping at the tail of the Helicopter causing the helicopter to slowly lose control. "Boss, the chopper can't take anymore. We gotta go!" Cerberus looks at him. "You dare to leave when we have them cornered and I will skin you alive." Cerberus and a few of his men would continue to fire below. But slowly noticed their ground forces were either killed, disappearing, or captured. A green gremlin would bulk up as he grabs Shadow and throws him onto the Helicopter. Shadow would grin as he soars through the sky and uses his claws to grab onto the helicopter. He begins to tear through the hull of the helicopter, his claws cutting through like paper. Cerberus would be confused by the Helicopter smoking as it starts blaring alarms. The helicopter spins as Shadow tears it apart, crashing into the constructed wall. Silence would fall onto the farm as everyone looked at the helicopter. Markus would walk towards the helicopter. The pilots were killed in the impact. A man with a scar on his cheek, blonde messy hair. His face looked familiar. "Fuck. Fuck fuck fuck! Boss, get up we-" Before he could finish Shadow would leap onto the man and force him to the ground as he stood on the man's body, soon bowing to Markus. "Master, he is all yours." Markus keeps walking towards the helicopter. Cerberus would slowly get out of the helicopter and stand atop the wreckage. "Seems the HellHounds are finished." He says as he pats dust off his suit and straightens it. "Well if we are to disappear then so be it. However you are coming with me to the gates of hell." Markus laughs as he raises his hand and prepares to snap his fingers. "I am afraid it will end how it began. You and me, but first. I want you to pay for your sins in other ways." He snaps his fingers and a dozen Gremlins Leap onto him as they pull him down from the helicopter. He freaks out for a moment as he falls over. He shakes a few off as he lands and then grabs a few and throws them away. The longer he struggled the more would come to bring him to his knees as they claw at him enough to leave a scar. Soon he would be brought down to his knees as the Gremlins held his head and forced him to look to Markus. "You are our prisoner. You will never escape. You will tell me all I desire to know." His eyes turn red. "And you shall beg for mercy and none shall be given." The Gremlins would carry Cerberus into the Farmhouse putting him in a dark part of the basement. Cerberus would yell and struggle the entire time. "KRONOS! WE ARE NOT FINISHED!!!!" The Legion would watch as the HellHound Leader was taken away. They felt pride and relief that their war with the criminal underworld was over as they cheered. Celebrating their victory, they would begin chanting the name of their leader. "Kronos! Kronos!" Their chants would give Markus Pride and comfort. The people would be free of the fear of the criminal organization. Though something tugs at him. He feels that there is something missing, something that made him think. Why did Cerberus go to his school, why did he steal so much money? Why was that scared man at his father's company? Are they linked? So many Questions rushed into his mind as his relief turned to tension. He turns to the blonde man under Shadow's feet. Walking towards the man, Shadow gets off the man as Markus grabs him by the throat. "Who are you? What is your place in the HellHounds? What is your purpose!?" The man spits at his mask as Markus's red eyes glow with fury. He slams the man into the helicopter. "TELL ME!" A few of his men walk over to see their leader questioning the man. One of them walks over to Markus. "My Lord. what is wrong?" Markus would throw the silent, stubborn man to the ground before the knight. "I need information… I need you all to do one more thing. I am not sure this is over. I need eyes and ears in every corner of the city. Find their bank accounts, their business partners, their allies. All of it." The Knights would be concerned, looking at the blonde man before them. Two knights grab him and drag him to the barn, into a makeshift prison. The Legion would trust Kronos as he freed their home, but worry within the ranks rose. A common question would ponder in their minds. "What could the HellHounds have done and why does Kronos need information on it?"

CHAPTER

20

CONNECTIONS

After the assault on the farm was concluded with a Legion victory, Markus would stand in the basement with Cerberus before him. Markus' eyes glow a heavy red. Rage filled his heart. The man who killed Sasha, the man who took his life. Cerberus would be shackled to the wall, scars from the gremlins cover his body. He makes no complaints, nor movement. Just staring back at Markus with equal hate. A single man who managed to be a problem, a symbol against his underworld criminal empire, a monster in human clothes. "You know. I might be named Cerberus, but you." He laughs before looking Markus in the eyes. "You are a demon, a monster. How you came to be real and gain such power is eye opening. Makes me wonder if gods are real. To think I would take the name Cerberus just to be met with a real demon." Markus just stares at him, angered at first but then laughs himself. "Even I am surprised by the mystics. I was just a simple student, a little more money in my pocket than most. But the day you took the name I gave you, things got… interesting." Cerberus raises a brow confused. Trying to remember any living people who said Cerberus from a school or maybe one of his own. "Confused? I figured." Markus takes his mask off revealing the familiar face to Cerberus. "No. I-I killed you. I broke your neck and dropped your cold body before my feet before the escape. How are you alive!?" Markus would laugh as he sat on the ground. One knee up to hold his arm out as Markus speaks his story. "Yeah I died. But my Gremlins gave me life and now I can't die. I am sure you heard the rumors from the Titan Creed. Most are true. Some exaggerated, but hold some truth." Cerberus would glare at Markus. "You are a corpse with power. Yet you beat me. This is a joke." Markus scoffs, getting up and putting his mask on. "I want to know why one of your Lieutenants was at my father's company. But first Shadow and his brothers will have a little fun. Break your mind so the words come out easier." The yellow eyes open in the darkest parts of the room as they all close in. Cerberus would do his best to maintain his manner and strength while deep down he wanted to scream for someone to help. Markus would leave the room. Shadow would watch over Cerberus using a few Gremlin lives to keep him alive as they ate him over and over. The torture was slow as he would scream and watch as he is eaten over and over. Markus would walk toward the barn as his eyes turned back to their blue. His Knights allow him in as they salute him. Walking towards the scared man being interrogated by a few Knights. Another would come in from behind Markus. "My Lord, I have great news. Commander Buck and Greg captured the last HellHound holdout. Even captured a few for your judgment." Markus would look at the man. "Excellent, inform our Commanders to return here with the prisoners and inform them to search HellHound records." The knight nods and gets to work on it. Markus turns to the interrogation. As soon as the Knights left the pen they gave their report. "He won't say anything useful. He was a delivery man for a bit before joining Cerberus, but that is all we know." The other scoffs. "Lord Kronos can learn by himself. See his guilt." Markus would look at them noticing a dependence on him. "No. There is a chance that he would not know if it was illegal. As far as I can tell it shows me their guilt and crimes from their memories. Maybe he did something for Cerberus without thinking it was criminal. Do what you need to get any information from him. If You can't, then I can try." "Of course my Lord, if the others get anything specific we can get the rest out." He nods and looks at the blonde man before leaving. Walking back to the Farm, he thinks about all that happened. How it all started with his death in his own school. Though thinking back to that moment confused Markus. Cerberus was in his school. A school with hundreds of teachers and students. The same day his own father demanded him to stay out. The scarred man in his father's office. Turning around and walking to his truck, getting in and driving off towards the city.

Later on he goes to the mayor's office and looks through properties and construction projects under Mars Tech Corporated. The dots start to line up as he finds everything on MTC. It had a contract to build a basement. It went over budget for a while. Then he sees that the cargo ship with the human trafficking was on a MTC registered ship. MTC was also trying to buy Tonka's club a few years ago. The amount of connections between HellHound bases and operations crossed with MTC too many times. Markus' eyes glowed red with fury as he threw the file cabinet to the floor. "How... why? What has father been up to?" He thinks and then gets an idea as his eyes turn back to blue leaving the building during the drive back he gets a call from Buck. "My Lord. I have found a lot of backroom deals on Cerberus' personal computer. However they are all cryptic and confusing. I get the basis of these deals. But they ensure the names are codes. They just call each other numbers." Markus was confused as he drove down the street. His mind spreads out to connect the dots and get an understanding. "Do you know how many of these numbers there are?" "No my Lord. Most of them are between 3, 5 and 6" Markus thinks as he gets on the road towards the farm. "So there are others? Another three at least. Strange. Why use numbers? Is it to hide themselves from each other? No it has to be part of their plans. Keep their providers silent." "Perhaps my lord." Markus would be in deep thought, thinking if his Father was part of this. Perhaps they used him or blackmailed him. He could not believe his own father would condone such evil, such corruption. He would return to the farm and march, with a concerned and angry posture, towards Cerberus. Cerberus would be terrified his mind broken as his eyes show a Terror unknown to any human. His body seemed to degrade and get thinner. Markus walks up to him and holds his face. "Who Did you work with!? Who did you steal for? Why are you using MTC stuff!? HOW DID YOU GET ALL THIS EQUIPMENT!!!?" Markus shouts as his rage shows. Cerberus flinches and shakes in his grasp. His mind was too far gone to be of any help. Markus backs up and takes out his pistol. "You don't deserve a quick death for all the pain and death you brought. For all the Corruption you are sinking in. Talk and I will grant you a quick death." Cerberus pulls on his restraints and looks at him with fear and yet a hint of rebellion. "You want the truth?" He laughs "I might be broken… but that will barely compare to you. Your Father is our partner. He joined our Order and he supplied our goals." The fear in his eyes starts to flee as he feels he wins this mental battle. What he did not know was this gave Markus the power to finish the fight. His eyes turned Red as he looked down at him with rage. "Father is one of you? Very well." Without hesitation Markus lifts the gun to his forehead and empties a bullet into his brain. Cerberus dies with a smile before the shadows drag his body into the darkness. Markus' blue eyes return as he walks towards his room and undresses down to his pants and sits confused and angered. He spends a couple hours thinking of whether to ask his father himself, to punish him, to see if he will ask for forgiveness. He wonders what had become of his father and the company he had wished to take over and move towards a better world. He would fall asleep thinking of it. His head on the table as he spent time looking out the window.

CHAPTER

21

FINAL STOP

Markus would wake in the white room. Standing up to look around, his bed vanished within the white room. Looking at the Blood filled floor, a huff of shame leaves his mouth. "If you can't handle it, then I will do it for you." His other half says in the mirror. Markus steps towards Kronos looking into the red eyes. "I will not give control to a monster." He turns away. Under Kronos' mask, he smiles and then chuckles. "I am not a monster, Just have the drive and purpose to fulfill our dream. Our Duty to this world." Markus turns confused and angered by his association of them together. "Our? Not our, they are my dreams. You have no duty... you are just a monster placed in my head." "Oh no I am you, I am the new you. I am Kronos. You are Markus. I was born when you were Reborn. I am the One who can help you get your dream." Markus would think for a moment, his thoughts were sporadic. Kronos sits on a throne that appears behind him. "How about a deal? Together we meet with your father. Your body will be ours for 24 hours or until we learn of your Father's part in this atrocious act." Markus would stop thinking and look at Kronos. "And what if the worse was true?" "Do not worry. Let us hear his words, then decide his fate." Markus steps over to the mirror and puts his hand out to seal the deal. "We hear from him. We decide here and whatever comes from it will be the results of the deal." Kronos smirks under his mask, rising up and grabbing Markus' hand. His arm crossed over into Markus' side before slipping back. He sits back onto his throne, turning to face left of Markus.

Waking from his dream, his right eye was red and his left was blue. Markus sits up and looks at the sunrise. He could hear

Kronos in his head. "So Shall we meet the big man?" "I didn't know that world was real. So you really are a part of me." Kronos laughs. "I am and it is real. However I just gave you the rage and confidence to enact. Though sometimes you did open a way for me to get out, yet with a rope attached." Markus would shake his head as he woke and stood. Taking his clothes and putting them on he makes his way out of the building without anyone seeing him. "So what of Shadow? Is he allowed in that world?" "No. That world is just our mind. Humanity has yet to unlock their mental world. Where do you think dreams come from? Our own reality. It is just ours. And the statues are the values we hold." Markus would stop next to the gate and think about that. Kronos was silent, letting him think. He stops thinking and walks to a car. Driving into the city was a quiet long drive. No music, no calls, only the clouds gathering to block the sun for a stormy day. Arriving in the City he parks the car in a back alley and uses a dark tarp to cover and conceal the car. Markus climbs the building and gets to the top as he looks over to the MTC tower. Jumping from roof to roof and cutting across roads as best he could he would arrive at the base of the building. Staring at the doors, One eye burning red with hate, the other soft blue with hope. He would soon learn the truth. One way or another. "Shadow, come to me." Shadow would arrive and bow his head. "You called, master?" "Indeed I did. We need to enter the CEO room atop of this building in silence. Cause some chaos with security. Oh and inform me of anything interesting from the data logs." Shadow nods and enters the shadows once more. Markus would climb down the building and drop off the 3rd level before rolling into the front area of the building. He walks into an alleyway on the side of the building. Towards a security door in the alley. It unlocks as he arrives at the door and opens it. Walking into the security room. Soon taking turns and hiding between walls and in rooms before making his way to the stairs. Within no time he makes it to the top level. Shadow appears on his shoulder. "Master, I am afraid there are Special guards ahead. They wear some dark uniforms with black masks marked by numbers." Markus would look to him with Kronos speaking in his head "Perhaps it is time we kill these guards. They likely work for this group that Cerberus was talking with." Markus moves to the door and peaks out. Seeing some men in black under garbs and dark blue jackets and stripes on their pants. They also had complete black masks with a series of numbers on their foreheads. "Interesting. I guess we should kill them. They might leave us no choice." Kronos huffs with annoyance. "You guess? They are in league with criminals. They are willing to kill and take what they want." Shadow walks onto the other side of Markus' shoulder. Yellow eyes peeking out to see the men. "Master, they are not men. They are monsters like us. Killers like Cerberus. You must kill them." Markus would step away thinking. "We shouldn't kill here." Kronos growls low before he bursts out. "Why is it a problem to do it here!? They are our enemy, they stand in our way! Besides, It is the only way to get the Information we desire." Markus sighs and nods before looking to Shadow. "Kill them. But leave no trace of blood or bullet holes. Not a single thing that suggests there was a struggle." Shadow nods before walking into the shadows. Some lights flicker before muffled screams are heard just barely. The Gremlins would grab them and snap their necks. Markus walks over to see their masks. Both had numbers on the top. "5-3019 and 5-3008, Maybe this is an idea how many there are?" No one responds as the Gremlins drag their bodies into the shadows to disappear. Markus then walks down the hallway. Before any of the guards cross his path they are ambushed by the Gremlins and killed or dragged into the shadows. Walking past the Secretary's desk, Markus walks into his father's office. Two more guards were relaxing in the office and noticed Markus entering. They move to attack him with batons. The room had little light from the windows Shadow and a few Gremlins leap at them and bring them down beating on them as they yell with no one to hear them. Slowly dragged screaming into the shadows. "Master. The Floor is secured. Not a single guard alerted and no blood or trace of us." Markus nods. "Good. Very good Shadow. Now keep the doors covered. Only the Secretary and my father will be allowed to live... unless by my hand." Shadow nods and leaves through another shadow. Markus would turn to his father's desk and walk over to the chair. He runs his finger along the desk, feeling the clean polished surface. He turns the chair and sits down looking at the desk. "I once dreamed of sitting here, forging the future by providing food, medicine and other needs to people. Creating a light in the dark times of our world." Turning in the chair to face the windows opening the blinds a crack to see out into the city. "To think this city was suffering so much, I never noticed till it hit home. I guess no one really cares what happens unless it affects them." "It does not matter, The City is liberated from crime and the Creed are gathering followers and rebuilding this city to be great." Markus leans back into the chair placing a hand on the chin of his mask. "Perhaps we can do the same for the rest of the world... Starting with this state. Then to the United Unions of America. Finally the World. Peace will be in every corner, united and free of pain." Both remain silent as they look out the window.

Hours passed, the top floor quiet until the elevator doors opened with Markus' father, his secretary, and a few guards putting on masks. The guards move to check on the others, splitting off one by one into the other halls, into death. Gremlins silently take each one, making their kills quick and unseen. While the Secretary takes her seat with a nervous look, Mr Mars and two guards walk into the office. Mr Mars would walk to a coat hanger putting his coat up. "Damn it, That meeting was a waste of time. We all know what happened and who is to blame for the loss of one of us." "Mr. Mars, what happened must not continue. I think that was the point of it. We are to lay low and keep eyes off you." Mr. Mars turns around and gives an angered stare that sends cold chills up their backs. "I am no fool, if you want to keep them from finding me then go secure the upper levels. Stop the elevator from getting up here and secure the building entirely if you have to. My future work will not be stopped." The guards move back uneasy with his glare. Then the guards rush out of the office to secure the elevator and upper floors, but only to find death awaiting them. As the door closes Mr. Mars takes his time to calm down and walks to his desk. Markus had heard everything and spoke clearly and calmly. "Welcome, dear father, to your office. I do hope there are some misunderstandings here." his father's eyes widened in shock as he froze up before speaking in authority. "Who are you? What are you doing in my Office? Guards!" "That is how you greet your dead son?" Markus turns around in the chair and stares at his father with blue and red eyes, his anger starting to boil to the surface. "Your guards are dead. Though I find it odd that YOU would be working with such a horrible partner. Though What is our policy on crime? Innocent till proven guilty? So father, tell me I was mistaken, tell me you did not work with Cerberus." Mr. Mars would grow angered. "You are not my son, He died a long time ago, how dare you! You who pretend to be the boy I raised!" Markus laughs then glares at his father before removing the mask. His father would be in shock, stumbling back before stumbling over his words. "You. You are alive? How? The doctors said your neck was broken so badly there was no chance of saving you even if they were on the spot." Markus places the mask on the table. "I am not alive, nor dead. I am not even sure if I am undead. But my friends gave me this new life. The power to fix the wrongs that Cerberus has done. Or you might know him as Number Three." His father, being too shocked to even think, speaks honestly. "Number Three wasn't supposed to kill anyone. He was just to get the money for our next project. It would be the last time I used his services. The project was to be sold to the military for a large sum. Money for the Order and for my company. It would have made me rich beyond those of this world. Then You could take the company and do your dreams without worry from the Order." Markus slams the table. "You worked with a criminal! You let him kill the innocent, Selling slaves and drugs to the people of our own city! To where the slaves go and come from

I have no idea. However, you allowed such evil to continue and sided with it! I would rather burn this tower down than work from such dark roots." Markus' heart was breaking with rage and betrayal. His own father allowed such horrors to happen without a second thought. The pain was unbearable, yet Kronos spoke with Markus. "He should be punished. Since he was your father, I am willing to give him a quick, but terrifying death." Markus looks to his right. "I don't want to know." Within a moment Markus stood in the white room with blood covering the floor. Holding his heart and head. "How could he? He could have helped the world. But his own desires and greed got me killed." Kronos looks at him from the mirror. "You have a troubled heart my friend. I propose a deal. Let me take control, Let me build the future of humanity. Let us destroy evil and sin and give the people a new age. A better future. Let us unite the world and bring this pain to an end. All I want is for you to help me when I need you." Markus looks at the blood his feet had sunk into. Growing tired and having no motivation other than to defend the people who entrusted their futures to him. "Fine. You can have control, Kronos, but I will watch carefully. We are partners." Kronos stands and laughs putting his hand through the mirror. "Deal." Markus would take a breath looking at the statues to his left and right. Both were degraded and were close to crumbling. He turns back to Kronos and grabs his hand. The deal was struck, while in the real world Mr. Mars would see Markus' blue eye turn red. Kronos was before Mr. Mars. Kronos closes his eyes and takes a deep breath in through his nose before letting out a large exhale of freedom. Opening his eyes and giving Mr. Mars a cold stare. Putting his mask on and standing. Mr. Mars would feel frozen in Kronos' presence. "Mr. Mars, Your Arrogant ways have led you to this moment. Your Greedy ambitions and path to power and death. So. Tell me who you are working with." Kronos would walk over to Mr. Mars who was frozen with terror in his eyes. "You. You are not my son are you?" Kronos stands in front of the shaken man. His eyes filled with rage as he stared into the terror filled eyes of a dead man. "You did not answer me." Kronos pulls his arm back and rams it into Mr. Mars' gut, sending him to the ground, gasping for air. "Tell me what I want and I will release you. No jail time." Mr. Mars would feel compelled to talk as the words poured from his mouth like the breaking of a dam. "We are part of an Order of powerful and ambitious people. Each one of the top ten are specially given a role in the Order. Example I am Number 5, I give the Order money to do our business. I am also the supplier of items and weapons. I do not know the others by name or what they do. I only worked with Number 3 because he was helping me Keep that money coming. Number 3 was in charge of the underworld. Supplying illegal items and weapons. Even procurement of people for the Order." Kronos would glare at Markus' father. "Your son would be disappointed. You would turn the world into your own puppet for greed and this Order?" "You don't understand. The Order's goal is to rule every sector of the world. From crime to Politics. From Weapons to cures. From the people to the Nations. We were to keep the balance of power. An endless struggle between everyone. To ensure no one has the upper hand other than us." Kronos grabs him by the throat in rage as he moves to the window and bashes him against it, cracking the glass greatly, but not breaking it.

"You seek to keep chaos going? To turn brothers and sisters on each other? You are not human, not even a monster. You are a creature of evil. Worse than my Gremlins. Not sure there is a name for you." He thinks for a moment before summoning a word. "Demon. That is what we can call scum like you." Mr. Mars struggles in his grip. "You said... You would Release me." Kronos would let him go as Mr. Mars gasps for air and coughs. "I did. I will release you. From this world!" Kronos sidekicks him out of the tower, forcing him through the cracked window and plummeting down to the ground. His body slams into a Limo parked outside. The End of Mr. Mars and his sins. Kronos looked down the tower. Huffing before turning his gaze to a setting sun. "Do not worry Markus. The Dream will come true. The World will be one. Starting with the UUA." He crossed his arms as he stared into the dusk skies. The terror that Kronos filled criminals with gave rise to his Legion. His rule over the city had just started. His mind raced with plans to build an empire. One that could unite the world. One way or another.

Meanwhile, within the city at a Hospital. The beeping of machines would be steady within a simple room with flowers and get well cards. A young lady laid in bed in a Coma. The Clipboard on the bed had the name Sasha Edwards printed on it. Within moments her eyes clench close before she slowly wakes to a new world. She slowly and weakly sits up as she looks out the hospital windows into the city. A silence filled the room only to be interrupted by one word from Sasha. "Markus."